FLIRT:

The Interviews

FLIRT

THE INTERVIEWS

LORNA JACKSON

BIBLIOASIS

FIRST EDITION

Library and Archives Canada Cataloguing in Publication

Jackson, Lorna Mary, 1956-
    Flirt : the interviews / Lorna Jackson.

ISBN 13: 978-1-897231-38-8
ISBN 10: 1-897231-38-5

    I. Title.

PS8569.A2645F55 2008   C813'.54   C2008-900198-2

Readied for the press by John Metcalf.
Cover photo by Daniel Wells.

  Canada Council   Conseil des Arts
for the Arts   du Canada

ONTARIO ARTS COUNCIL
CONSEIL DES ARTS DE L'ONTARIO

We gratefully acknowledge the support of the Canada Council for the Arts and the Ontario Arts Council for our publishing program.

PRINTED AND BOUND IN CANADA

for Lily

Contents

I Flirt with IAN TYSON

—You smell like a saddle.

—Thank you. I appreciate that.

—Ol' Eon, they call you.

—Some do, yes, some did call me that. Will you accept a slug of Courvoisier in that mug of coffee?

—You are credited – no, thanks, you go ahead – you are credited with reviving the lost art of cowboy poetry and cowboy songs. The *Atlantic Monthly* called you the "leading voice of cowboy culture."

—Well, the men did all that. I'm simply the one pickin' and singin' and posin' for the nice liner notes. I'll calve the heifers at forty below come spring, but I'm no John Wayne or anything. It's not the money.

—I appreciate what you did for the men who rode the range. I appreciate your compassion for the Navajo rug. And I like your white hat. Maybe take it off.

—Not just now.

—What kind of dog would that be?

—Where?

—That black and white dog way out there chasing the mallard, over by the pond, the trembling aspens. See it?

—My wife's border collie. Somewhat haywire.

—Is it true you sang "Don't Fence Me In" at the funeral for the head of Woodward's department stores?

—My friend Chunky Woodward bred quarter horses up there on a half million acres at Douglas Lake. I owned the offspring of Peppy San, his world champion cutting horse, and I admired a man who could fly out of concrete downtown Vancouver Friday afternoon and scout the pine rail fence lines on his ranch, hike in bunch grass for all the weekend. I was honoured; folks wept in that big church, and that's good.

9

—Ever shoot a Hereford steer in the brain with a rifle while it's eating grain, and then cut its throat in your frozen brown field, your daughter's watching NBA basketball on TV, two days after your forty-fifth birthday?

—I know those who have, old cowpunchers; no one like you, though. Grief is unpredictable. I estimate it's a figure eight, a riata.

—When I first heard the songs – *your* songs, not yours and hers – I was new in Vancouver, back from card cataloguing an Indian Reserve school library, enforcing the Dewey decimal system, decorating walls with good-natured book jackets. Kindergarteners were flaccid from marshmallows for breakfast, canned icing. The kids there wondered after the clean bandages around my wrists. "Did you cry," they asked. "How *much* did it hurt," they wanted to know.

You have a daughter, the one who was little and blonde in that rug video.

—A young lady by now, I believe. I believe she paints.

—Back in Vancouver, city chick reborn, I fell hard for a sax teacher, fell hard for an Athletic Director, fell hard for a Restaurant Manager. Then I bought spike heels and a cameo choker and dumbed down and fell for four guitar players in a row and stopped at Danny. He had your records. He had a jumbo Gibson and extra-hard picks; he had an apartment in the East End off 12th Avenue.

—Could do worse. Could date stock brokers. Women like you, though: legs, dark hair that curls. Musicians. The mix is readymade and often too strong. You have no enduring regrets, I'm hoping. You've moved on, apparently.

—A band party had made me nervous. I dressed too filmic, flirted chaotically. I drank many somethings and pretended Emmylou with her Hot Band. I imagined all the boys wanted me but respected my music so much – my "approach" so much, the legacy of Gram and legendary shit – plus the grey starting through one side of my long hair, that the boys could only be pleased when I strummed their knee with my fingers. The skinny drummer from Steinbach. My hose shredded. I swooned. Danny got me out of there, walked me off to his apartment against the coldest night, and tucked me in under his mother's cat-piss afghan.

Four a.m., still dark, he served a plate of buttered toast and scrambled eggs with hot salsa. I came around – magically nude – to the stereo playing. He wore a scruffy brown bathrobe, open to the waist. Cartoon hair tufted at his sternum. And the record played you, Eon: "Surely to goodness –"

—"This time . . . it's forever."

—Uh-oh. Might weep a little.

—Well, that is a lovely voice you have. I mean it. Just don't Emmylou your lyrics. Don't swallow the words, sweetheart. Hey, . . . wait. Hey . . . Hey . . . You still with me? Show me your pretty face.

—Look at that little dog. Look out there. Her dog's just running circles out there, pressing down the low hay, disappearing into it, happy to be crossing your huge green field, duck or no duck. I hear a chainsaw. Do they call you tenor or baritone? Is that vibrato natural?

—They call me, as you pointed out, Ol' Eon. He's pretending sheep.

—You're much, much older than you look.

—I thank you again.

—Danny handed me a beer stein of cold grapefruit juice and stretched out his long legs beside me on the mattress and said, "You need someone to look after you," which was both true and false.

—Like western music.

—Maybe. Danny opened for you with his buddy Stan Mitrikas, first at the Golden Garter Saloon in Edmonton and next at a paddock folk festival outside 100 Mile House. They were eighteen. Danny'd just left home – Thunder Bay and a drunk-choked dead brother – and they called their set-up The Luminators. Telecaster, Precision bass, tick-tock drum machine.

—I don't recall anybody's drum machine.

—He worshipped you, but you've heard that before.

—Picker boys. You understand their weaknesses as well as I do, evidently.

—Now, is it "One Jump Ahead of the Devil," where you confess, "My pickers are about to leave me"?

—You've got the tune. And they always were and always did. Still do, given the right direction of wind and adequate velocity.

—Why is that?

11

—Why is what?

—Why are pickers always about to leave, why do they do that always?

—Well, at one time I was probably not the easiest person, not the easiest boss or bandleader. I refer to relationships with certain painkillers. Likewise, Lightfoot, the Hawk, likewise the world. I have known hard-pressed freelance steers and my legs betray those battles, my hips in particular. The ankle was rodeo-shot long ago. Pills.

—I wrote a paper in grad school – this is way past Danny – about you and Leonard Cohen.

—You'll have to lead me through the connection, would you?

—Cowboy poets. Mellifluous.

—I'm not seeing it. Good grade?

—I was pregnant. I was broke. I overlooked how Cohen, given his ethnicity, his pricey Montreal tailor, his haircuts and angel choir, is more rodeo clown. A cowboy parody.

—Parity is important, especially in a relationship. Or a record deal.

—Who's your tailor, Eon? How do you get that thing to happen to your jeans, where leg meets torso just like that? Don't be shy. You are the most handsome man.

—In showbiz?

—In everywhere. Danny would have hitch-hiked all night into any crevice of any province if you'd called to say, "I need a player." Three years into us, he was playing the lounge of the Newton Inn in the botched end of Surrey. You were booked into the cabaret. At seven o'clock, while he was doing a high and heartfelt parody of Kitty Wells, you limped into the lounge and had a few kind words with him. "This is my girlfriend," Danny said. "She's a singer, too."

—Now, tell me I didn't make a pass. And if I did, I'm here to say I'm sorry but I've always had an excellent eye.

—I was twenty-five and puffy at every joint, my face a scabbed balloon. I doubt it. You asked him to join you later on the big stage, to sit in on standards, sing some backup, the high harmonies. Danny knew all the notes, all the parts and possibilities. Hundreds of hick couples scuffed around the dance floor. Cigarettes were legal and the cloud cover was low. Later, after

Danny sang with you on the stage, naked and gangled without the Gibson and its wide strap, me and Danny danced close to the high stage. He wanted to just go home. The women curved beneath you, but so did bolo-tied men. They all wanted your eyes to follow them, regardless of Stetson shadow.

—Danny. Still playing the bars?

—Nashville.

—Good.

—We're all thrilled for him. Stan electrocuted himself in the bathroom at the Hope Hotel, maybe you heard. Plug-in radio. Deliberate act of "fuck the world."

—Well.

—Can we talk about "Summer Wages"?

—That came a ways before the cowboy songs.

—Of course it did, but it came back on *Cowboyography*.

—What did you think about that album? Be honest.

—Oh. Nice fiddle, the piano a little tinkly, thin sound overall, backup singers too angel-choir for me. And yet perfect, too, for all those reasons. The remix of "Summer Wages" was apt, given the album and its larger context.

—How so?

—It seems to me many of the themes and images and tonal patterns that show up in the later cowboy songs – I'm thinking here of the more lyrical and swooping melodies of your romantic ballads – existed, too, in "Summer Wages."

—Not sure I follow.

—Come on. Men. Work. Cowboy pride. Women for pleasure not forever. The solitude of physical labour and the dislocation of seasonal employment. The unexpected melodrama of the minor chord. You're not seeing these as recurring patterns in your work?

—Could be there, I confess. I call them "knife and whore songs." They're not for everybody.

—The hookers standing watchfully are symbolic of the stands of cedar timber, and vice versa.

—Hold on. Not so fast.

—Hey, I've *lived* with a towboater, man. I've *seen* the women outside the bars on Main Street. The Waterfront Corral. I played those bars and I saw the boys and their pay packets thrown up in the alley. I sang "Someday Soon" and saw losers fall in love on the dance floor of the American Hotel. The steel guitar sliced my inner ear and when the serious clapping faded and the hicks stuck their fat tongues down each other's throats, Charlie the Steel said to me and my voice, "See what you do? See it? You make people do that to each other."

Is that a Calgary Stampede belt buckle?

—Austin, Texas. Home of the armadillo.

—Now, I thought they wouldn't let you back into that country. Some warrant in some state. Do I have this wrong?

—I've been pardoned.

—The towboater had never heard your lovely logging song.

—Not surprising. Lousy radio play in those days. Still. We have entered the age of the big black hat.

—So after our first weekend together –

—This is the towboater, now?

—Right. After the dozen croissants and pot of coffee and Seattle news-papers, I stayed naked, slimmed down and smooth, and took out my old Yamaki –

—Hey, they made some nice instruments. What year?

—Bought the year my sister died, with the 150 bucks left in her savings account. I've had guys offer one grand, cash, for that guitar, even with overweight heads and cracked neck and warps. Deep. Big. I developed a style of finger-picking – part pluck, part slap and pull and strum – that gave extra bottom and punch to the slimy folk sound. Where my fingernail hit the sound hole there was an ugly rip in the in-lay, but the sound was good, percussive. I played for the towboater, facing him where he propped his sore neck on three pillows. I sang. He didn't know where to look. Embarrassed, shocked. Tired, I suppose. He said he liked the part about "slippery city shoes" since he'd just had a pair – 400 bucks, custom measured – of caulk boots made. Have you heard what they call it? "The folk scare of the early seventies."

—Parts of it were plenty scary. You never smoked, did you, not with skin like that. Is my leg okay there? I need to stretch.

—I'm forty-five years old, Eon. I am grieving the death of my womb.

—I'm told there is a serenity, a kind of pasture mentality. I mean this in a kind way. Forty-five is too old for a cutting horse. Horses should be frisky, good blood. Ambition. Forty-five is just about right for a woman. I predate you by decades.

—You married a teenager. Leave the leg.

—You fell hard for the towboater.

—The towboater came to Christmas dinner at my mother's townhouse at the mouth of the Fraser River six months into our, let's call it, relationship. He'd run a load of logs across the strait on the 21st, towed a concrete barge the 22nd and worked the booms for twelve hours after a bundle broke loose as the snow flew on the 23rd. His hands could hardly hold the cocktail fork; an old scar defined the numb tip of one finger; maybe he wasn't keen on shrimp. On the third round of wine, my mother's new lesbian hippie friend – Julia – leaned at him all shrill: "You are killing trees that are better off *blah, blah* . . ." "I just tow them," he said. "Nevertheless, you are complicit in the murder of old growth," she said. "How do you know how old these logs are?" he said. "You objectify them with that term – 'logs' – so you can feel okay with being the vehicle of death." Then he said, "Already dead, they're logs. Still in the ground and standing, they're bait. Economy. They're the walls, you stupid dyke."

—Maybe I like this fella.

—That's your first smile of the day. We drove home upriver to New Westminster. We sat outside the apartment in the little front seats of his tiny Renault –

—A guy like that drove a Tonka toy? Don't date guys like that, sweetheart. You're looking for someone with access to four legs.

—He did not cut the engine. He reached across me a little way to that stupid door handle and shot-putted it open. He almost didn't make it back over to his side; he was that drunk he had to push himself up off my knee. But he glued his hands onto the steering wheel and pretended the Indy – fast hard turns and jerking the wheel to miss ad hoc barricades – *rrrrrrtch* –

and he said, looking out the windshield and up at the streetlights, "My family is funnier than yours. My family is smarter than yours. And my family is better at sex than yours."

—The end?

—Not for long. Now, do you have to shave twice a day to come out so smooth? Smooth as Perry Como.

—Only when meeting media.

—Mind if I touch your face? I've noticed you have a thing for women with three-syllable names, peculiar consonants: Sylvia, Beverly, Juanita.

—Shirley.

—Ever play with a drummer named Lou?

—Sure, probably. Can't see him, but I probably did. Lou sounds like a drummer's name.

—Here's a good question: How are drummers different from pickers?

—That *is* a good question and I'll try it. Drummers drink scotch, while pickers fill up on draft. Drummers like hard-core strippers, while guitar players prefer the bartender's girlfriend, or maybe the part-time hooker flogging long-stemmed roses after midnight. Drummers typically bathe several times a day, whereas a picker will wait for the weekend or maybe the next.

—Lou hung himself in the Hope Hotel.

—That's a bad joke.

—No, we all played there. Lou didn't make it out, either.

—Let's walk.

—Oh. No. I don't need that.

—Yes, you do, you need to walk.

—What's your favourite crop?

—I mean it. Let's walk. We'll be the dog's flock. Those shoes are fine. Wear my big sweater. Put the pencil down.

I Flirt with BOBBY ORR

—Your knees are like Popeye's biceps after spinach.

—I can't get slacks that fit.

—I've never been in a Cadillac. Does this one have a name?

—Escalade.

—That's a pretty word for a car. A pretty idea.

—I had a Corvette years ago. I love them, they're beautiful, but I have trouble with my legs, so getting in and out . . . getting in and out of the Escalade is much easier. I wouldn't call it a car.

—"He has an Austin's motor in a Cadillac's chassis."

—Who does?

—They said that about Jean Béliveau. Six foot three with a Tin Woodsman's too-small heart. Drive, Bobby. Should I call you Bob? Now, do they still call you Bobby?

—Some do. The fans, the fans' kids, the bogus websites. To them, I'm always twenty-two and flying through the air. Call me what you want. Not on the floor; there's a trash can in your armrest.

—I hope I don't make you nervous. Just drive. I suppose you're a defensive driver. Get it? Defensive? Your hands are trembling like a compass. What's that steering wheel made of?

—Leather and wood. It's already starting to change with my hands. See there? Like a putter, or a hand-me-down axe. You should know I'm scared skinny of talking like this. I'm no shucks as a talker. Don't do that. I'll turn up the defog, but please don't use your hand. The grease.

—I've lived in apartments smaller than this car. First time away from home – 1974 – off to the university across the water, I rented a little bachelor joint down 82 stairs to the rocky beach on Shoal Bay in Victoria. That's 82 down and 82 back up.

—That's 81 more than I could handle.

—Even then? Even the year you scored more points than Esposito? Than everyone?

—Especially then.

—Me too, turns out. I'd had a bad fall in 1969. January, the streets of Vancouver fluffed with snow, and after school the rough boys – the Meraloma rugby players, the boys I liked, their cowlicks and white teeth and ski jackets and perpetual running shoes – chased us with snowballs in the wide-open frozen streets, between cold-arched chestnut trees. I ran hard – I was twelve, long-legged and fast, happy to be chased by those boys – and then I slipped on the hidden ice – a boy named Paul winging an ice-ball at my bare head – and fell to my knees and slid hard and fast into the curb. My kneecap hit first. My elbow hurt most, but when I tried to get up a whole joint had disappeared.

—Sports injuries often happen this way: you think it's one limb but that's a trick, turns out to be another. Prompt and professional diagnosis is key to successful rehabilitation. Now, did you shatter it, crack it or what?

—Stay with me, Bobby, you sound like a pamphlet. Cracked across. Swelled to three times by dark. I lay in the den with my leg on pillows, my mother annoyed, inattentive, chain-smoking Black Cats, rum and Cokes; our dog barked at icicles falling from the eaves. My older sister was giving parts of herself to Hodgkin's Disease. My father was missing.

—Missing what?

—In November 1968 – two months before my fall – he had disappeared, left a note in his Pontiac Parisienne under the Burrard Street Bridge saying gone for good – suicide – and . . . Don't worry, Bobby, don't do that with your eyebrows: he came back, it's not like that, the story's not sad, he sat out a season, that's all. He had a little Soldier's Heart, a little Post-Traumatic Stress from WWII and a crash in Germany, a little Shell Shock come back to haunt. Lost his memory, lost his way.

—Let me know if that heat's too much on your feet. I need cold on my legs; the Escalade can do both at once.

—How many people can you get in here?

—I've had eight adults but that's without golf clubs.

—My father was missing when I cracked my kneecap. And my mother couldn't manage one more complication, a girl like me: injured and cold. Another body's degeneration. She didn't consult a doctor until the morning of day two. Then a night in hospital. Drain the fluid, full plaster leg cast for a month.

—They'd never do that now. Too much muscle deterioration. Now it's a system of braces.

—My right leg is a quarter inch shorter than my left.

—Back problems?

—You bet.

—Parents have to take a more educated role in watching out for their kids' bodies in sports. Fundamentals. Codes of conduct. Early sports injuries can ruin lives and limit an adult's activities later on. Coaches, too, must condition their athletes from day one. Sorry, I'm a pamphlet again. You and your father were close?

—Pliny the Elder spoke of knees as symbols of power. They've been called "the knob of the head's staff." Do power brakes help with your legs or make it harder to control the stops?

—Sorry. I thought that guy was coming off the curb. They help. But still some rough stops. You know, no one dies from knees.

—Howie Morenz: dead of a broken leg.

—The game's changed.

—In the 1969-70 season, four years into the league, you won the scoring title – 120 points – you won the Hart Trophy, the Conn Smythe, and your team won the Stanley Cup. You scored the winning goal in overtime.

—Derek Sanderson was in his third year with us. Your dad would remember him checking Béliveau.

—I know; I'll get to him. The next year – spring 1971 – my father – recovering from amnesia, from his time missing – was a Canadiens fan. He had always loved Jean Béliveau and stressed to me that Béliveau was the sort of player – the sort of man – we should all admire. A handsome gentleman, no naughty elbows, the home game sweater, the *bleu-blanc-rouge*, a little grey at the temples of his shot. Béliveau's last season and that year my father fell for Ken Dryden, his attitude, how he knew everything, could stop anything. The McGill law degree, the clean face, the wiseman posture: chin on glove on stick. A tender. I took the Bruins, I took you and the black shirts and Sanderson's urges. Four is still my lucky number. Lucky for what, who knows, but I like its heft, its girth and smooth sound. I hear the number and see you – your shoulders not huge like the boys now – your face clean, hair flying, and so much neck in that vulnerable golf-shirt way, no Bobby Hull farmer tuft at your neck. My father in the big chair, feet up, his slices of sharp cheddar and Labatt's Blue and the sports section, rubbing the shrapnel starting to surface in his forearm, the game helping him back to the present. Me on the loveseat with my long teenage legs crossed, a springer spaniel's head at my knee. My sister upstairs purging chemo. The Canadiens took the Cup that year.

It smells like a saddle in here, Bobby, but quieter. I'd count the speakers if I could find them. In the doors? On the ceiling? Merle Haggard never sounded so buttery. *We'll have roses in December . . .*

—That's a pretty voice you have. It's the old country tunes I like. Not too jumpy, but not too smooth. You know, except for Hull, no one had really big shoulders back then. Now players do more to bulk up, spend short summers training and pumping. All we had off-season was lawn-mowing, golf and the race track. The game's changed and their proportions are different, muscled, not bulk. And the equipment adds inches.

—You were handsome, regardless. My father was missing, suffering – we learned later – from amnesia in a hotel room on Vancouver Island in Nanaimo. Occasionally, our phone would ring and he'd either be on the other end, talking like nothing was wrong – "I'll be home after work" – or he'd groan into the phone and scare me. The cops put a tracer on our phone, but I don't remember the premise, the rules. The night I was in hospital with my kneecap, he phoned my mother. She told him she couldn't do this bullshit (my word, not hers), that I had broken my leg and she'd had enough. The hospital staff was to watch for him; my sister somehow got my mother's cream-coloured Austin running and sneaked into the kids' ward with daffodils and a chocolate milkshake from White

Spot car service, ten at night. The next day I was home. Soon, so was my father, sick and tired of waking up sick and tired, worried for my knee. The start of that 1969-70 season.

Five years later, the little apartment on the beach down the 82 stairs? I moved out in four months and that kneecap could not stay put.

—A flight of stairs is torture. Too much weight set on that disfigured joint. Get me an elevator, or I don't go.

—Before I fell, I wished for a broken leg. I'm telling you, but I haven't told anyone else. I wished for something interesting to happen, that would make people care about me in a serious way. I guess twelve years old wants attention and I wasn't getting my allocation.

—Lucky I never had daughters.

—Back to 1974: sister gone in 1971, the year the Canadiens won, Béliveau's last game. I quit university in December 1974 and dumped the boy from Sociology who resembled Sanderson and, no muscles to hold it in place, my kneecap kept slipping and sliding and locking. I had surgery the next September.

—Not another cast?

—Standard then. Sub-luxing patella. You know the details. The night before surgery, a cute intern fondled my knee, front and back, and asked if I'd taken ballet as a child. He said my kneecaps sat up off the tracks like someone who'd pressed her legs too far back.

—I think you have nice legs, especially in little boots like those, but I wouldn't say ballerina. Swimmer, maybe.

—That's nice for you to say. I'd played volleyball in high school, and I dove for balls, tried to out-crash my best friend. My father suggested it was time to quit the game when my shoulders and neck began to resemble Bobby Hull's.

—Fathers don't talk like that now.

—There's a theory, you know, about competitive sports and its reflection of a phallocentric culture, of orthodox masculinity.

—Tell me some of it, but stop if I say so.

—It's about self versus other.

—I follow.

21

—Competitive sport demands that the masculine colonizing urge conquer the space of an "other" while protectively enclosing the space of the self. Isn't that the definition of an offensive defenceman? Heading across the red line but still ready to hold your own blue line? Or sexual desire coupled with the need to be as manly as possible.

—Okay, but if that's your metaphor, it seems obvious.

—All right, make it sexual. The player whose desire to win produces the most invasive phallus, called offensive strategy, coupled with the tightest asshole, defensive strategy, wins the game.

—Stop.

—Nietzsche called it a festival of cruelty. Look at the Greeks!

—Stop, I said.

—When my father saw my muscles building, the risk to him was that I would join – visually and sexually – the masculine realm of sports. But there's only one way for women to be both phallus and asshole.

—Be lesbians?

—According to this model, yes.

—That would be hard on a man like your father.

—He loved Peggy Lee's ankles.

—And Jean Béliveau. Tell me about the rehab after your surgery.

—Bobby, I was nineteen.

—No rehab?

—I was depressed.

—You sound like a goalie.

—The exercises hurt. Come on. My sister was dead, I had one epileptic dog and two wrecked parents – "Don't upset your father" – and everything got dark, hopeless, loose and preventable. My mother didn't push me to work out. I remember bags of sand but only the occasional lift. I had no coach. The surgery – see the scar?

—Can't look now.

—The surgery punished me for everything. Who cares about walking when you've quit university and have to live with sad parents and be the daughter who isn't the one who died? Losing a quad muscle hardly seems significant.

That feels good on my face. How did you do that?

—There's switches for all the windows right here. I can lock your door, too. The passenger ejector seat was optional and pricey so I passed. I'm having second thoughts.

—That's a mean joke, Bobby Orr, but I see your point. How many operations on yours?

—Six on the left knee, going on seven.

—Now, they say you revolutionized the position of the defenceman in hockey by taking the traditional moves and blasting them open to drive for the net. Three strides, top speed, spinning past forecheckers, around the net and up to the goalie's open side. Scotty Bowman said for each possession you "took pictures" from your defensive position and then built a story.

—Scott said that?

—I added the story part. I think you were an astute reader. You read the game, recognized its patterns because you'd read so many examples so thoroughly before. You saw characters who'd likely follow a predictable course given their motivations, flaws, desires and limitations – and you found a way to enter and influence the story, to make it more poignant or thrilling, given existing patterns. Fast, maneuverable.

—I saw room, spaces. I wanted to keep the puck moving. I regret that my play made others seem inept. They weren't. Just caught out. You've looked at highlights packages and see goals. After a rush I knew I could make it back to defend my own end. But I didn't always. My style caused problems, believe me. I made mistakes that cost the team. Bad mistakes.

—You also became known for the behind-the-net clear to centre ice, where often Derek Sanderson would pick up the pass, you'd catch up and you two would kamikaze for a short-hand score.

—You see guys use that play today, but they don't get enough slick on the stick, and they turn it over in their own zone.

—My father wasn't keen on Sanderson.

—No, mine neither.

—The handlebar moustachio, the white skates, hair even longer than yours. Sex on ice, compared to say a Béliveau or a Cournoyer. I went through a Sanderson phase – revisited it when Dale Tallon played for Vancouver – but always came back to you. Remember the nude centrefolds of Joe Namath and Jim Brown in *Cosmopolitan Magazine*? I still have those.

—Derek always got the draw, and he practically invented the sweeping poke check. To my knowledge, he never sold pantyhose.

—He took the white skates thing from Namath, right? They opened a bar together next door to the Playboy Club. Sanderson said he was obliged to live out every sex fantasy he'd ever had.

—That would be plenty.

—What about you? I'm told – by a writer friend on the limp, a duffer hockey enthusiast sans gall bladder, a guy who visited your house when he was ten and saw the room where all your trophies lived, and noticed you being shy albeit a legend already, your freckles and carrier cut. He says you playing for Chicago was like a dog in leg casts and that you partied very hard one summer in a fish camp on the Sunshine Coast of British Columbia.

—Derek and I didn't hang out much, the occasional eighteen holes. I went to his bar a few times, but you could see the fall starting. It wasn't funny to see the addictions take his judgment. And we couldn't tell him anything, the coach couldn't crack down. Part of the power of the Big Bad Bruins was Turk and his excesses. The city wanted that almost as much as the Cup. They got both when Turk played. He was doomed and the million bucks finished him.

—Last week, our neighbour David's truck rumbles down the driveway, exciting my lab who loves his tennis balls and fast hands. He has sliced his thumb from tip to base on his new Australian axe. While he cut cords and stacked them, a wasp bounced up to his eye and took his attention. He tells me about the blood, the pain, the clamping while the mother-in-law called First Response, the new pain when the paramedic pinched where David had clamped, the Demerol's bliss. He holds his hand upright, like a surgeon ready for duty, and hangs it from one finger at the neck of his white T-shirt. A Bobby Hull tuft.

He has stopped in to show off the new kits. Wine kits. I hear the words and see the tidy boxes stacked in the back of his truck, my heart thumps and terror or desire rushes into my hands. Kits: young foxes, home pregnancy, Craftsman homes in cleaner times. Kits. "Those kits, they're top of the line, they're primo, they're like Chardonnay," he says, his chest big beneath the sliced thumb all wrapped in gauze.

It's been fifteen years since my last drink – a cold bottle of pear cider I guzzled the Labour Day morning before I trimmed the laurel hedge in Sapperton, went to the top of the tallest step ladder with hot and weak knees, began to cry and couldn't stop, couldn't climb down, couldn't fathom the branches I'd shorn, longed for a rough blade at my own neck.

"It's like Chardonnay," he repeats and wants me to treat him as our dog does, the huge and wet smile, the pissing on his sandals. I say, "I have no interest in this. I'm an alcoholic and I don't want to talk about this."

—Nice shot.

—"I think of it as cooking," he says, "but fair enough." I've known this man for eight years. I know his wife, his children, his beach-stink dog, his wheel-chaired mother, his injuries, trespasses, preference for breasts, his fishing holes, and I've dined on his smoked salmon; I know the colours of his dahlias, I know he can't get jeans to fit because he shears sheep and builds fences and his thighs, like yours, are Popeye thighs; I know where he and his wife first made love and that their lovely daughter was thus conceived, I know he wept the first day he left his boy to stay at our co-op preschool, I know he played trumpet once for Mel Torme in high school in North Vancouver.

How does he know so little about me? How does he ignore or forget the crucial detail, the one important pattern? When I quit, my friends were relieved and also put out. That's normal. But the worst betrayal: not one – guitar players, singers, funny people with large enough hearts – not one told me it was time to stop. Not one said, even sober, "ever thought of quitting? Don't you want to be happy? We love you, be well."

You had a reputation, Bobby.

—For?

—Puck bunnies.

—And the reputation?

—Circumference, length, vigor.

—History forgets I was twenty, scared skinny, a boy with a crew cut from Parry Sound. These are now my fifties, my legs have walked a century. They don't bend or take my body's weight. Pain always. I've earned and been robbed of a half million dollars. I introduced my teammates – strong boys who skated ponds and slow rivers and worked their uncles' butcher shops come summer and never finished high school – to sonofabitch Alan Eagleson. You talk about betrayal? I'll never make it up to them. That reputation you refer to – the details I still see when I don't want to – seems old and silly now.

—I stopped watching when you left the Bruins.

—You had other things to do.

—The game changed. My father stopped watching when the WHA salaries went stupid. He said he'd rather play golf than watch mediocre players make that much money. After his first heart attack, exercise became crucial and he went back to grass court tennis.

—If Béliveau was his man, I understand his disappointment.

—If the "neutral-zone trap" were an animal, what animal would it be?

—Pirhana.

—It swallows what?

—Momentum. Pride. The story of open ice.

—They build new knees, Bobby.

—So I'm told.

—My father and I watched that game, in May 1970, thirteen months before my sister would die. She will spend her nineteenth summer in Paris and die in St. Paul's hospital in Vancouver – pneumonia – the following June, after Béliveau and the Canadiens beat the Bruins in seven games to advance for the Cup. But the world of my father and me in the den in 1970, that world is still capable of ice and sports and naughty long-haired heroes like you. In that photo of the Cup-winning goal you scored in overtime – the trick and planned pass from Sanderson ("This is it," I said to my father as the puck came around and found you) – in that photo you are flying, Bobby. You're so up. You are a boy above the city, taking off and flying home to Parry Sound. Your wings are spread and there's no pain, your knees cushioned by the frozen air, and you will never need walking again. No more vertical. All is flight and victory.

And then you disappear; Sanderson – happy like a boy on sports day – slides in and lies on you, loving you, wanting you young, his hands on your face, that embrace. Men in love, so up. You do seem young, even now. Your hair has gone more golden than grey, along this line, at the temple.

—We're here.

—We are?

—Stay where you are. There's ice. Stay put. I'll come around and get the door.

I Flirt with MARKUS NÄSLUND

—Wait up.

—Come on, you can stay with me on water this calm. A kayak's about pushin' more than pullin'. You're pullin' too much. Firm the wrist. Push the paddle. Push.

—If I had triceps like yours I'd be zooming into Victoria harbour by now. I should've gone with the fiberglass like you. My shell's dragging.

—Push.

—So, that naggy groin's all good? The concussion, the bone chips are vacuumed and the cartilage cleaned out of your elbow? The scar over your eye still bothers me – did you not use cocoa butter? – but I suppose you're more hockey tough to look at. Any pain from last year?

—You mean physical.

—I do.

—Because I'm not goin' to talk about the other. You said I'd be able to breathe out here. You said you'd stay away from playoffs and scandals.

—It's your body I'm interested in. What was that look? Hey, come back here.

—I saw a personal trainer five days a week in the off-season back in Sweden. I'm thirty years old and in the best shape of my life. I want to win the World Cup.

—Markus, get real. The goalie situation: you can't be everybody.

—I've improved all parts of my game last year, especially in the defensive zone. I'm confident we can give Tommy more support in goal. Some saves – I'm thinkin' of Belarus, the Olympics – he shouldn't have to make. What do you call those birds?

—Those are cormorants.

—In Sweden, we have them. No: push. Relax those shoulders.

29

—Do you and Forsberg talk World Cup strategy off-season? Do you call each other on your cells and say, "Hey, Peter, when we play Canada, Mats gets the draw off Burnaby Joe and I'll outskate the old tractor Mario up the gut while you make your move down low on Jovo and then find me on the half-boards so I can scoot a wrister into Brodeur's slow spot"?

—We talk, but not like you. No. We'll keep it vanilla.

—Which means?

—Simple. Plain hockey. Honest hockey.

—You said once – before The Troubles – that Colorado plays honest hockey. Hey: don't look at me like that, not when the sun's bright and not too high yet and the water's dark and glittery and you can smell the Strait of Juan de Fuca on your hands already. The Bertuzzi glower. You didn't have it before. Two years ago, you're back from the broken tibia and fibia, the leg's healed and your hockey spirit soars, you're Mr. Honest Congeniality. You had time and sincerity for every locker room lens and cartoon-haired geek's mic even mid-slump. At the end of the season, trying to find more goals than anyone in the league but also trying to captain the team, you confessed – the smudges under your eyes, the sad red-knuckled hand through wet hair – that you'd hit bottom. No wizard can conjure optimism from anguish every time. But you knew buoyancy would lift you, trusted the physics. You'd hit bottom, apparently, but were coming back up. "I've been there, man," we all whispered to our late-night sportscast, "I've been there." That year, even in times of trouble, you wanted real communication. You wanted us all to chat and share woes and have a few laughs and then get on with the job. Celebrity did not yet gleam on your skin.

Last year, though, you're short with the press, your eyes are hard and Swedish blue, you don't smile or sparkle. It's like you and Todd, up in the hot treehouse with protein bars and Gatorade, scabby legs crossed, elbows and knees tough and black from summer, you naughty monkeys, made a blood-brother pact to be a couple of hard-ass jocks. I'm not one of them, but some people – the cranks who call into 24-hour sport talk – say you're not what captains should be. Strip the C, they say. No, says some caffeinated jerk, he has to do it himself, he has to give it up willingly, let's not have another Linden *coup d'etat.* Hey. Wait up, Markus.

Okay, okay. The kayak forces me to consider only your upper body, especially from back here. I thought hockey players were built like mailboxes up top, but no.

—The gear makes it look like that. Think about it. Forty-second shifts at top speed, full use of lung capacity. Too much muscle and the lungs can't inflate; and muscle weighs tons. Too much bulk and you lose speed. So lower body has to be powerful, but up top should be lean.

—Not out that way, Markus, we need to stay closer to shore. There's a towboat and we don't want to run over his lines. Those guys hate kayakers. Wait up, hey, how'd you do that? How'd you get there from here? Man, you're everywhere.

—More push, less pull.

—If we steer straight – go around that kelp bed – we'll get to the Haystack Islands and the seals will surround us. I imagine the Strait of Juan de Fuca is a lot like the Gulf of Bothnia. Same terrain, same climate. I don't want to hold you back, but I can't hear when our boats are too far apart.

—Similar, yes, the water is the same darkness, but where I grew up is more extreme. I played hockey outdoors, which no one can do here. Peter played across town indoors, of course. It was good when they came to play us because they hated bein' cold, havin' frozen toes, and we knew we'd win. We were much tougher than Peter's team. I'm sure he'd agree. Are you with me? What strength sunscreen do you have on your face?

—I'm good. I'm safe. Sorry to hold you up. Your father was your coach.

—Yes, my father taught me. And Peter's father was his.

—Man, I play tennis with my daughter in the shade of old growth fir on a hot summer morning, the clean breeze reaching up off the strait, our visors tipped against the dappling sun and spritz of pitch, our arms getting brown and our strokes – our ability to wait for the ball to drop to our waists – improving; old men in retro-whites play anemic but cheery doubles next court and discuss the updated stats of their hummingbird feeders and their wives' most recent blood test with accents both British and eastern European (Nick, the only one in a singlet) while keeping score and disputing calls ironically; the occasional diving shriek of a kingfisher, no pressure, just a smooth rally. Even there, tears end the session and they're not always hers. The game face of my daughter is a Bertuzzi scowl of bad manners and lazy psychology.

—Many times, my father would make me walk home from the rink because of my attitude on the bench.

—Would you do that now? Make your little girl walk home?

—He was always honest, my father. He always told me the truth. Your form is improvin' already.

—He said that?

—No, I'm talkin' about you. Your form is better.

—Yeah, thanks.

—You look more natural in the boat and stronger, too.

—Right, yeah.

—Bend at the waist just a little. Breathe in through your nose, out through –

—I know, I know. I work out. I can breathe. I'm old but not that old. They say fifty is the new thirty but that would be eighty in hockey years.

—It's true, though. This is a lot like home, it's relaxin' on the water and quiet without a motor.

—You have the same birthday as my dead sister.

—Hold up, I'm comin' back there. This fog will only last a few minutes. Let's paddle alongside each other. That way, I can watch those wrists. Firm them up, no togglin'.

—The water goes so smooth when the fog comes in. It's like the cocktail party's over and we're the only ones left in the messy quiet.

—Except I don't drink.

—Me either.

—That should help with your moods.

—What moods? Who told you that?

—It's only tennis.

—A writer I like, a Canadian turned ultimate New Yorker who still believes hockey is the greatest game, says, "We are optimists and look to sports to amplify our optimism."

—It's true. There's always a way to play better, always a new season to feel good about before it starts. Always a way, a system, to overcome obstacles – injuries, mistakes, whatever. I think fans look at us and see that we persevere and we show them there's hope, even when spirit breaks, or your leg or elbow, even when a best friend is broken badly.

—Now, I know you're a spiritual guy. Your dad's a pastor, right?

—Sort of.

—Ingmar Bergman's father was, too. You knew that?

—Lutheran, I think.

—Remind me to ask you about Bergman at some point.

—Oh, ya, you bet.

—And I know you don't want to tell me about how faith works in your life, but it seems so much a part of your game and your life. It's too bad you don't want to share your wisdom and help us all to maybe get along better and be happier and decide what's holy and what's not.

—Well, I'm a public figure but I'm also private and so is my family.

—Yes, but what is it about Christians that makes them so insider-ish? It's like they have a secret society and the rest of us don't get to come to the meetings. If it's so great in there, why can't everybody come in, chug a cold beer and a Cheez Whiz sandwich, and then leave?

—You don't have churches in the Strait of Juan de Fuca?

—Ha. I'm not talking about going into a real place; I'm speaking figuratively, I'm using a metaphor. It's *like* you people have a secret club and you don't want heathens to know what goes on there.

—I know what metaphor means. Answer this: in the playoffs, when they call us warriors, is that a metaphor or a direct comparison?

—It's a cliché, I know that much.

—Maybe look it up and get back to me.

—Let me think about it.

—You don't believe in God, is that what I'm hearin'?

—Here's what happened. I'm fourteen and I have a terrible crush on Davy Jones of the Monkees.

—He dated a Swiss actress. Ursula Andress. My father had her in a James Bond poster rolled up in his closet. I spent a lot of time in there.

33

—Okay. I'm fourteen and you're almost born, and I've been writing letters to Davy for a couple of years, trying to get an answer. First, here's a
question: Why do kids do that? Why do they want to communicate with
guys like you? Why isn't it enough to watch the games or, in my case, listen
to the records. Why the letters? Hey listen: foghorn. Kind of redundant.

—I think there's reasons. I think it's an emptiness – maybe just a small
hole, nothin' to worry about – that they're tryin' to fill. You had an emptiness to fill. You were lonely in a way that friends and family couldn't fix.
You probably should have gotten serious about soccer and entered some
tournaments – round robins are really great for kids and you don't need
expensive equipment – but pop music isn't a terrible choice. Do you want
me to name all the members of ABBA?

—My sister was dieing; she was twenty. Do you have any idea where
shore is right now?

—At fourteen, that would leave sore spots, for sure. Let's stop here until
the wind takes the fog. I can feel the sun. It won't last long. Lay your paddle
across my boat.

—So one day, my sister's on the loveseat, sick from chemo or radiation,
I can't remember which.

—What cancer are we talkin' about?

—Hodgkin's Disease.

—Like Mario.

—Right. But when my sister had it, nobody survived it or bought
hockey teams or skated again or made dekes or trick passes through their
feet. So she's home and somehow I know that today's the day the letter
from Davy Jones is gonna come. I *know*. We're in the living room in June.
There are antiques – a little George V walnut desk –

—Nice.

— – under the window overlooking the peony bed in the back garden,
gold velvet loveseats, a turquoise-blue Chinese carpet stained by our spaniels but still smooth, 1914 oak floors, a fireplace tiled in blue-green, teak
cocktail tables.

—This house was in what style?

—Georgian.

—Nice.

—Not fancy. My father was an auctioneer so he found stuff.

—Simple is often the most beautiful. Those birds?

—Buffleheads.

—I like the shape of their heads and how they all dive together. I wonder how they know to all go at the same time. Drink some of this; rest your hands.

—So it's this day and I've decided to stay home from school because I'm sure the letter from Davy Jones is going to come and it's early June and Grade 9 is almost done anyway. And I play double solitaire with my sister and sometimes she has to lie back on the velvet loveseat. She eats green grapes and drinks ginger ale to settle her stomach. She looks like shit, once lovely with black hair and twinkling eyes and smooth pale skin, freckles provocative and sweet across her small nose. She was entering a series of last stages. She'd been sick for six years, was supposed to last only two but science was moving fast and dragging her along. Not fast enough, obviously. But still.

—Family support?

—Support?

—Who were you talkin' to about the transition, where were you gettin' help for what the family was goin' through? What hospice?

—No such thing back then, not in this country. What?

—Really?

—Really. We were on our own, Markus, and no one talked about it.

—Why not?

—Private.

—That's ridiculous. What were they afraid of? Honesty is the most important thing. That makes me angry.

—Wait up.

—Sorry.

—Don't leave me in the fog.

—Sorry. What's that rumblin'?

—Freighter, but far away. So our spaniel goes nuts, as usual, and again I just know there's a letter. I wait until the mailman's gone down the stairs and I can see him cut through our side garden, jump over the little rock wall and skip up to the neighbour's house. And I open the front door – we've had to put the mailbox outside so the dog won't grab envelopes and shred them – and there's a letter from Davy Jones in a creamy envelope.

—But it's a form, a copy, not a real letter.

—It is a real letter. It refers to things I'd put in my letter. "You don't have to be a bird to feel the way you want to feel," Davy wrote, because I'd mentioned I'd like to be a seagull so that I'd be free and, like, eat seafood whenever. And I say to my sister on the loveseat how I think I believe in God now, because I was so sure the letter would come, and I'd been really praying for it and now, miraculously on the day I stay home from school, here it is. And my life is so great and this must be religion and God's in charge of everything that matters.

—That's not what religion is. That's not what prayin' looks like.

—Listen, I've seen you score a crucial goal near playoff time and look up, your stick still smoking, and thank God. I don't think that's what religion is either. The team – the boys, the fans – helped you score that goal, not God. And you're not supposed to talk to Him while we're all watching Sportsnet.

—What did sister Mario say about your sudden conversion.

—So my sister looks at me and with what's left of her burned-out brain says, "It would have happened anyway." And I know she's right. Maybe it's hindsight, maybe I'm embellishing, but I think even at fourteen I understood that a real God would not let my sister suffer for years and still feed me letters from a false God like Davy Jones and let me brag about it to my sister on the velvet loveseat. "It would have happened anyway," she said, already through with any idea of a benevolent God for herself. I was being asked to choose: you can have a God and Davy Jones and the cheap-thrill pathetic world of short celebrities from Manchester dating busty Nords, or you can have the respect and intimacy of your smart, beautiful and doomed sister. No contest.

—But since then, once the grief was less painful, surely you've been able to realize that –

36

—Nope. Since then I've been on my own. Hey, no fog. Wait up. So Markus, Mr. Nike multi-millionaire, what false gods do you worship? Do you agree that hockey is the religion of this country, that you are one of its gods?

—I like jewelry. And I like my belt to match my shoes.

—There's no one in the NHL who looks as good as you in Armani.

—Well, I don't know about that.

—Okay, not counting Trevor Linden.

—Trevor's four inches taller than I am, his legs are longer and he's quite a bit older.

—More saint than god, when you think about it. I wish all you guys would go back to wearing eyeglasses. Look at Larionov in his wire rims. What a doll. Hunk city. Laser surgery robbed the sport of true handsomeness.

—I see those islands. Let's go out a little further. Keep talkin', we'll go easy.

—I asked my doctor a while back why an older woman, say in her mid-to-late forties, would suddenly be taken with hockey players. Suppose, I said, a character in a story fantasizes about hockey players, sees herself helping them plant rhododendrons in their Shaughnessey garden or attending dress-up events at the Bayshore with them and looking sleek and young, imagining they're interested and wanting her in the cart at charity golf games. They're bored of the hockey-blonde wives they scored in the bars in Juniors or the loyal, lanky girlfriends they wed post-high school. They're ready for a wise woman with a sense of humour and a sense of occasion. I asked my doctor, is there a physiological reason for such a state or is my character on the cusp of a more humiliating stage of peri-menopause?

Libido is complex, he said. Perhaps she has a precipitous drop in estrogen and progesterone which allows testosterone to take over. Or, he says there's a study: they sprayed male sweat into one bathroom stall and left the adjacent one clean. Sure enough, most women peed in the sweaty stall. We're naturally attracted to the hormones. Sure, I said, but my character's not smelling these guys, she's watching them on TV. Still she wants to go

37

out and buy fancy underpants and jeans that dip below her navel. She wants to curl free weights, cross-train elliptically, so they'll notice her jiggle-free arms and be lured. My doctor says there's a Pavlovian response under those circumstances, where she sees them play, sees them on the bench and interviewed in the locker room and she associates them with the sweat. Also, he says, there's probably some disinhibition happening because the screen makes these guys seem safe and also available. Which, I guess, they're not.

Or are they?

—No, they're not.

—Okay, okay they're not. But why do you think a woman would think that way? You must get groupies.

—Your doctor knows best, but I think it gets back to that emptiness we talked about before.

—She doesn't feel empty, Markus. She feels full and alive and young and ready.

—Yeah, but she's bein' unrealistic and tryin' to be someone – what's the word? Implausible. She's pretendin'. I don't know a player out of the 700 I play with who would be attracted to the character you've described. *Maybe* Chris Chelios. Uh-oh. Stay still. Don't panic, just push on the sand bar with one end of your paddle and try to keep upright. That's it, push yourself out this way. Now you can touch bottom with your hand and push away from the bar. Okay, maybe not. Grab the end of my paddle then. Hold on and I'll pull you off.

How did you end up way over there?

Let's go find those seals you promised.

You're lookin' so sad. I'm gonna tell you a Swedish fairy tale to cheer you up. My little daughters love this one. It's about a man named Red Roderick of the Seals. One night Red Roderick was fishin' on a rock an' he heard the sweetest music. It was so sweet that he followed the sound until he came upon a musician playin' and a bunch of people dressed in fancy clothes dancin' to his tune. Close by, in the moonlight, he saw bundles on the ground – black and white like cowskins. He tucked one of 'em under his jacket.

Eventually the music stopped an' the dancers went to their bundles of skins, threw off their fancy clothes an' put on their hides. They all turned into grey seals. They flopped over the rocks an' swam out to sea. Except one beautiful girl. She rushed around frantically lookin' for her skin, cryin' and sobbin', clutchin' and grabbin' her hair.

So great was the girl's beauty an' so pitiful her cries that Red Roderick was taken with her, smitten, an' he asked her what was wrong. She said she'd lost her garment, an' Roderick said that if she would go with him he would get her a much better garment in town, which he did, even fancier than the dress she'd worn to dance.

Red Roderick's feelin's for the girl increased. So a priest was found to baptize her an' they were married an' reared a family of children. At last, however, the girl became lonely for her old life, her friends, an' the dancin' an' singin' in the moonlight. She asked for her sealskin back. The seals, she said, wouldn't touch her because of "the blessed water on my face an' forehead." Then she asked that her husband never kill another seal for fear it might be her. Red Roderick agreed an' that night she danced in the moonlight with her old friends, although none would touch her. An' she swam away with them.

That one behind you looks like Mikka Kiprusoff.

—What?

—Like Kiprusoff when he tilts his mask back from his face, after a save or after a goal, doesn't matter. He resembles a calm wide-eyed seal, breachin' the surface, to consider those poor mortals stuck back on shore.

—They're everywhere. They're all around you. They love you.

—Listen to their breathin'.

—How do you stay so optimistic, Markus, even through shattered fibia and tibia and rabid press who ask you to be yourself and then hate it when you are, and through terrible losses and desperate and tormented friends and so far from home.

—The toughest thing to cope with is not injury, it's uncertainty. My wife's taught me a lot about stayin' calm an' positive. She has all the patience I don't have. An' my kids always have a great outlook. They've shown me the power of sheer innocent joy. It's hard to be depressed when you're around little kids.

—My sister died, of course, and five years later I was living in a fishing village at the top of Vancouver Island. My then husband was a lay preacher for the Anglican church; he had stolen my skin so I couldn't dance.

—That's a nice use of metaphor.

—He was a fisherman, and one day my parents drove the long and dusty logging road to visit and brought my sister's ashes with them. We all took the box out in his little fish boat. The waters of Johnstone Strait flow and reach around the world and this idea made us happy, that my sister would be so international. On a calm Sunday morning, we set out with the box of ashes in my husband's green wooden lobster boat.

—Wait. There's lobster here?

—Converted boat.

—I see.

—He knew the strait and took us far from the bay out to the right spot. There, my mother opened the box and, with the boat coughing along at trawling speed, emptied it into the water and said good-bye to her favourite daughter. Some ashes blew back and lodged in the trim along the boat's side; I leaned over and flicked them into the ocean. As I did, a school of bright silvery fish came to the surface roiling all around the boat, thick and deep, and as they did, the engine cut out and the wind came up. We floated and bobbed as my husband tried to re-start the engine. How many minutes, I don't know, but when the fish were gone the wind went flat; the engine caught and started.

That scene probably means something to you.

—Of course it does. It should mean somethin' to you, too. It should mean you never have to feel alone or dismayed because there's always a higher power with you, showin' you the way, leadin' you through fog and into the clear. Makin' contact.

—It would have happened anyway, Markus.

—Sure. But imagine somethin' more.

40

I Flirt with ALICE MUNRO

—Do you smell chicken manure, Ms. Munro?

—The market's full of smells you don't get in the city. It's the smell of work and rich soil and humus. It smells like simple, plentiful life. You'll like it when we get to the berry tarts my friend Johanna makes. Every Friday night – from the first of the rhubarb to the last of the pumpkins – she's up till three in the morning and then awake again at six to get the baking done. Imagine working that hard at something. Call me Alice, won't you?

—Man, it must be a hundred degrees out here. I wish I'd worn a hat like yours. I like how the straw makes your face sparkle. You had three kids and a husband in a beige city. Still you managed to write your first collection of stories, some of the most powerful stories by anyone, any time.

—Well, my girls would nap –

—Jesus, Alice. I'm so sick of that anecdote. Can't you give me something better? More honest? Something that doesn't make us all feel like slugs? When I started to write stories, coping with a bipolar pregnancy full of worry and woe – in my mid-thirties and blooming late in all regards – I read that you'd written *Dance of the Happy Shades* while they slept. I took comfort. *Well,* I thought, *that seems okay.* The baby will sleep and I'll get at it, I'll write the best of my prose, full of deep feelings and great details. It will be a lovely internal time. And then I'll be patient when the baby wakes up, because I'll have had creative fulfillment for the couple of hours, peace, and then I'll dance with baby around the kitchen singing Supremes songs with "baby" in the lyrics. Art heals, you bet, and I anticipated this new, better life, its riches.

Anyway. One critic says you are able to compress without miniaturizing. Comment?

—Here, have a plum. This will knock your socks off. Bernie gets these off a tree planted by his great great grandfather, Jeremiah Glover. He's

41

given everybody grafts, but no one's plums taste quite as earthy and sweet as Bernie's.

—He has a crush on you.

—Oh, no.

—Yes, he does.

—Well, I see what you mean – the thumb and forefinger to the cuff after he takes my money, the left eyebrow raised slightly instead of hello, the other hand in and out of the back pocket, and obviously the spitting into the handkerchief, that's sexual. No harm, though. People flirt, that's all there is to it. Maybe it's flirting you smell, not manure.

—I'll get a bag of those plums on our way back. Even the colour seems too good. So the baby's born: gorgeous. And I cheer up quite a bit, even though I'm living with the staff writer for a local weekly who keeps hideous hours.

—This is the baby's father?

—Right.

—You should be more precise.

—The baby's great, and after some breast-feeding problems –

—Such as?

—Well, the latching on was flawed, the midwife didn't catch it, so blisters and cuts and excruciating pain whenever the little fatso wanted to feed, every ten minutes or so.

—What exactly did that feel like?

—Stabbing.

—Stabbing with what.

—Okay, stabbing with a chainsaw.

—That's not possible.

—Exactly. And not only did she want to stab me with a chainsaw every ten minutes, she did not nap.

—That's not possible.

—You're wrong about that. Bedtimes were good, no problem. But she would not nap during the day and for the first four years, she'd be up with your friend Johanna at the crack of dawn. So she'd get cranky and floppy by afternoon, and I'd put her in the crib in the little room at the back of the house and play a sugary lullaby tape and do everything right, I swear. She'd let me leave the room, make a cup of Earl Grey tea and find my favourite ultrafine felt pen. I lowered myself into the couch, laid my favourite pad of tiny-lined paper across my knees, and took my first look out the picture window to see what the world had to talk about. "Come get me, you slut," she'd whimper, wail, yelp. Time's up, no art today. Every day was like that.

—Surely your husband –

—Not married.

—Surely your man would give you some time?

—I hated art by six o'clock. I was the one at home, and our story was looking pretty traditional by this time, so dinner was up to me.

—Weekends then. He takes the baby to the park for a nice swing and you scoot up to the library on the bus while the washing machine's running.

—Listen, Alice. If I'd really *really* wanted to be writing at thirty-five with a newborn I could have figured out a way to do so. No debate. I know it's possible to argue that I was a lazy, whining, good for nothing loser mother who couldn't sweep the floor without getting sad. Women writers in history who made the most of their brains and talent and kept writing: the list is long. Kids got diseased and still the 1000 words a day. I know. I'm just saying, you set me up to expect one kind of life with that write-while-they-sleep bullshit anecdote. And I got another kind of life.

—But the stories came eventually.

—They did.

—So it all worked out.

—Okay. Hey pooch.

—Those are Bernie's dogs. They'll follow until we get to the organic dog treats then head back. The little one seems stuck on you. See the man selling tomatoes, the one with the dirty grey ponytail down his back and the rotten teeth?

—He's got a dachshund under his arm and the hair on his chest's coming up in a nice tuft from the blue shirt?

—That's him.

—What?

43

—Roy. His wife Stella teaches at the university – she might be Associate Dean by now; no one tells me anything – and you wouldn't believe how few weeds they have in their two-acre garden. The Muscovy ducks help, but she's out there in her coveralls every evening from April 1st. She just published a startling 900-page encyclopedia of disappearing languages in the several South American countries she's taken her kids to – no, the youngest four. The eldest two are in South Africa working in the townships, something to do with AIDS and cooperative housing. You have no idea. Look at the green of the basil next to the red of the tomatoes. I'd like a silk blouse with those colours.

—I suppose you still write all day every day and find time to stare out the window with a cup of great coffee for, say, eight hours.

—You seem angry right now. You do. Look, you've annoyed the dogs. Have I said something accidentally to make you so angry or are you one of those women who's angry all the time? I suppose it could be the heat. You don't get this humid heat in British Columbia and the linen probably seemed like a good idea this morning but now you're finding it sticky around your underarms. Still, it's pretty for a day in the country. Or maybe you've got a bad hip from the sports you played as a child, and the market's big enough and we're doing so much walking that you've got a little pinch just above the coccyx and you're having trouble feeling pleasant. Your hip flexor's tight. Let's take our muffins into the shade and sit. Better? Yes. Now. Was this your first marriage-type relationship, the one with your baby's father?

—I was married once – I made my own dress (a million pencil pleats) while working in the elementary school with a predominantly aboriginal student body and looking after a springer spaniel with epilepsy – when I was nineteen.

—What decade are we in?

—That was the late seventies.

—An interesting time to be a woman. Feminism had offered some answers but the questions were growing more complicated.

—And there seemed to be so much work to do on the whole culture to make it even close to worthy of the name "democracy".

—Where to begin when you figure out you've been getting privileges others only dream about?

—What's that spice?

—Not a spice: orange rind.

—Of course. So I was in Alert Bay at nineteen, married to a schoolteacher who was also a lay preacher in the Anglican church on the reservation and who fished commercially on an Indian boat in the summer.

—There's lots of material in a character like that.

—I'm not sure we should pick a mate on that basis.

—Maybe not, but the better the nouns, the better the marriage. Describe his hair.

—Oh, whispy blonde and then white in summer, the tideline climbing further up his forehead. Bright blue eyes.

—Blue like sky or blue like ice?

—Blue like heartache.

—How did the Indians take to him?

—When we moved out of the manse on the Reserve to a cottage at the other end of the island, a bundle of them came around in a big ugly pickup while he was at work and stole his firewood from where he'd dumped it in the driveway.

—He'd chopped that himself, I suppose. You'd fall for a man like that. A woodcutter.

—Despite his allergy to yellow cedar.

—You should drink that juice. Rachel presses the carrots and beets in a very nifty stainless steel juicer and then adds last year's frozen pulp from her late spartans. Can you taste the ginger? Special ingredient: cantaloupes, also from her garden. Let me tuck this in your blouse or you'll have the whole spectrum down your front.

—Thank-you. Your skin is so smooth.

—Drink. Here's that little dog back to forgive you. I wonder what made his tail go so crooked. That's a lot of wagging for such a small dog.

—Long story short, the school year ends and the new husband goes fishing.

—So soon?

—I fall for someone, anyone and husband comes back from a coho opening and the someone's wife finds out. New husband says, oh yeah? He wasn't really fishing but down in Vancouver with Sandra or Susan or Sally, arranging for the birth and adoption of their child.

—You knew?

—Nope. I knew he was infertile according to the last sperm count. So he said.

—No.

—So he'd fooled around before we got together and now the baby was getting contracted out.

—You were nineteen.

—So young to figure these things out: guilt, betrayal, hostility. I was living on the water and the trees across the strait were old, huge and lush. The closeness of landscape did things to my common sense. Up there, it supernaturalizes emotion, lures the mopey and allows them to disconnect from what matters. Green on green on darker green. My dog was so neurotic she couldn't cross the road and scout the beach without a chaperone.

—Your dog's name?

—Thurber.

—Oh dear. Life should be lighter when a dog has that name.

—I was out of love and set on this other woman's husband who seemed set on me but also on his wife, who was a hotshot and deserved better; I was working in the library at the school; and my sister was teaching there.

—Oh, for heaven sake. What a thing to do.

—Yes.

—What a mess of complications you managed to scramble together. And with an epileptic spaniel, too. Violence, or the implied understatement of it?

—Well, he threw a knife at my head as I sat on the couch.

—Miss by much?

—Oh, he meant to miss. He hated that knife because I'd cut strawberries with it and never wipe the blade which, he said, would cause corrosion, pit the blade. He didn't like it when I let the emergency brake rub teeth when I pulled it up, either. That, too, would wear things down.

—There's a metaphor to put on the list. So. You're a teenager and a man is throwing a knife and there's a wife about to get even – how did you escape this tangle, as if I have to ask.

—You spend half the year in Comox.

—Yes.

—Then you know the hospital there, the one with the psychiatric ward?

—Yes.

—So they pumped my stomach and stitched my wrists –

—What was in the stomach?

—Turpentine. Champagne.

—I wonder if that kind of corrosion would permanently damage a stomach?

—I wonder, too. The doctor said, "We don't want a woman who carves and poisons herself living in our community. Come back when you're ready to be part of the community." And the next morning they flew me down to Comox in a little Cessna 180.

—Seems like a hypocritical thing for a doctor to say. After all, I'm sure there were worse than you in the seventies in a place like that.

—Tough love?

—Nonsense.

—It was a good time to leave. I remember not much.

—Memory is a very interesting organ. I bet if you started to write a story – not autobiographical, but personal – about that time, I bet you'd begin to recover details and feelings and events. They'd be suspect in their accuracy, of course, but you'd have them.

—Not yet. I'm not hungry for those details yet. And the story seems sort of bewildering and pathetic. I was wrong about everything.

—Oh, the story could work around that. Give that young woman a little more power, blonder hair and a head scarf, or maybe set it in the sixties, and really work out the landscape so the story's also about that, and I think you'd have an interesting moment to play with. But these things take time, you're right. A story can't always be squeezed out of history. With me, writing has something to do with the fight against death, the feeling that we lose everything every day, and writing is a way of convincing yourself perhaps that you're doing something about this. You're not really, because the writing itself does not last much longer than you do; but I would say it's partly the feeling that I can't stand to have things go . . . Speaking of hungry. There's a Dutchman down the way who makes divine sausage and bakes his own sourdough buns. He usually has a bottle of Kenyan beer tucked in a cooler under his tailgate.

—It seems to me your stories are getting sexier.

—Well, you may be right. Hello Harry! He's handsome, don't you think? His wife's arms jiggle and she talks about her sons' PhDs too much. Still.

—Most of them begin with a paragraph loaded with female desire, female want, some naughty language. And later that desire is mocked, then refused and finally satisfied in some way.

—What story are you thinking of?

—"Floating Bridge."

—Of course. You would like that story, given the lives you've led.

—I love that story.

—I do, too. But tell me why.

—For all the right crafty reasons: the invisibly-stitched physical description of characters; the ambiguous relationship between the cancerous woman, Jinny, and her asshole husband, Neal; the plottiness that has become a bit of a pattern in your later work whereby a caregiver or nurse – a third party – is introduced into an existing relationship; the class-conscious settings of paradise and its opposites; your weaving of present and past. I love it for your skill, is what I'm saying, and how you manage to dance so much so fast, without your tights getting saggy.

—I'm not sure that metaphor quite works. But add it to the list.

—And because I'm getting older and because men . . . I, but they, we – well, the ending.

—Ricky's kiss on the bridge pleases you, doesn't it.

—It really really does. When the boy drives poor Jinny home – they've only just met – and he stops and they look at the stars on the bridge. She's forgotten her hat in the corn field and she has only a nob of a head. He touches her waist and kisses her. He says "oh." I asked my friend Johnny why Ricky kisses her.

—Oh, I'd like to hear a man's opinion on that.

—Johnny's not just any man. But he said, "What's in him at that moment? I don't know, some bizarre cocktail of bravado and compassion and oedipal urgings. Why does he do it? Because she wants him to and he's a good boy. Because he's so alive he's bigger than death. Because he's on an Experience-gathering expedition, and this is a Big One. Because this is where he brings girls to kiss them, and she's a girl. Because they've slipped out of the stream of time and become ageless. Because he's so beautiful it would be a scandal if nobody were kissing him. Because he reads her well enough to know he can get away with it, and getting away with things is the teenager's *raison d'être*. Because he's in awe of the moment he's concocted, and knows he has to do something remarkable to mark it . . ."

—John's words comfort you, don't they.

—They do.

—Why do you think he kisses her? Before you answer, try to open your mind, your heart, try to think about where you are – in the country on a hot day and eating a handful of blackberries that will stain your lips, holding my hand like we're girlfriends off from school for the turning-point summer we've been waiting for. Look at me. Now, why do you think he kisses her?

—Feel this under the dog's front leg. Here, Alice. Put your fingers under mine. Feel that? There's a little tumor under there, floating around, fixing for trouble. But look at him, smiling in his sleep, oblivious. Good dog.

He kisses her because she gives him the word "tannin". No woman has given him a word. Take off your hat, Alice. He kisses her because she's beautiful regardless of time. Because he can't help it.

49

I *Flirt with* RICHARD FORD

—Waiting for you to phone feels like high school. Will he? Won't he? How do I look?

—But I called, whereas in high school they likely didn't.

—I went to high school in Vancouver and stood far too many cold afternoons under the colonial street light on the corner of Wiltshire and 43rd with boyfriend X, after our respective rugby and volleyball games. I tried to convince him I wasn't too crazy to love long term, that just because my sister was near death I wasn't sad all the time, I could tell a good joke, cared about the civil rights movement and necked well, though ancient at fifteen. We stood so long my toes froze, in sight of my square blue Georgian house, its rhododendrons, my mother's cream-coloured Austin inept in the driveway, but we didn't go in there. X helped keep me whole but by graduation, he had taken up with a rough covey of rugger chicks who liked their boys straddling rebuilt Harleys with long scars where pins held their ruptured bodies – elbows, knees. Girls who drank hard liquor fast and smoked weed in their parents' condos at Whistler and took pills and called that carefree. My sister dead, I quit the team, and found a nice United church redheaded boy who refused to fuck but could fingerpick a punchy acoustic guitar – his brother's D-28 Martin – and who lived for the scratch and squeeze of tight harmony. Of course, moral differences ripped us apart, and the phone calls stopped coming when I begged the world for one more talk. Richard, this is already better than high school.

—We'll see.

—Thank-you for calling.

—My pleasure so far.

—You may occasionally hear the sound of chickens. My office looks out on a rough little coop built seventy years ago from field stones and cedar shingles by a local shoemaker and is now home to a dozen Barred Rocks and a couple of freakish and testy Black Minorcas. Their egg yolks this time of year are a yellow not otherwise found in nature and taste rich as French pastries, thick from a diet of hatching slugs. Early this morning, turkey vultures circled low and shadowed the windows Hitchcock-wise. I found the hens stockstill, like a watercolour, huddled under the tayberries. The rooster – a huge and handsome Barred Rock, his tail a conquistador's helmet – posed on the nearby pathway, ready to give it up for his girls, to be their he-man. I urged and flicked them back to the coop and fixed a board across the hole they'd excavated under the run's wire. The vultures circled and watched and dipped close in their primitive formation and then sauntered off. Today, all day, the rooster will crow. Your voice sounds sweetly Southern and bourbon-soaked. Am I right?

—It's only noon where I am. What a peculiar question.

—Are journalists asking you different questions this time?

—I just kind of started, last week, so the questions seem quite fresh. They don't seem to be questions about "does the landscape influence your work," "Do you have a problem writing about women," "Why are your men kind of western guys?"

—Has your celebrity changed the tack we're taking?

—I don't think celebrity lasts very long, frankly, so I'm unaware of that. For the most part, when people ask me questions they're quite nice, and I can usually get my head into them. They aren't frivolous and they aren't dumb. Particularly in Canada, I'm always pleased with the kind of preparation journalists do. Much better than in the US of A.

—Well that's nice to hear. I am not only a journalist, though, and my questions will arise from several positions: writer, teacher, critic. Your writing showed me many things when I started working with the sweet calisthenics of the short story. I like men who are kind of western guys, maybe that's it. If my questions seem odd or random, they are, and they need to be.

—All right.

—You have written so incisively and compassionately about father/son matters; one of your most-quoted lines is that the best thing a father can do for a son is die. What's the best thing a mother can do for her son?

—Mothers are much more, by and large, nurturers toward their children, and that was the case in my life. What I wanted my mother to do was survive, that's the thing she didn't do long enough. I wanted her to live on into both my adult life and her later life. And I guess the other thing that a mother can do for a son is not hold his gender against him.

—Here's what I think you meant: fathers have too much control over a writer – a male vocation according to you – when they are alive. Men are always trying to tie the silk tie like their fathers could, or mow the lawn at the correct height given climate conditions and density of ranunculus. And when fathers die, a world of feeling and perception becomes available: quit cutting it, let it meadow. Be yourself.

My mother held my gender against me, too. The tight red jeans she called dreadful; haircuts with too much angle or sheen, dreadful; menopausal symptoms in my thirties, nonsense. She suspected every man of wanting sex from me and nothing else, suspected that I encouraged them. The choir director who made us sing Benjamin Britten's tone cluster of twelve-part harmony; the grade seven teacher who explained Mussolini and taught bluegrass and drilled me – perfected my forearm pass to eliminate the need to fall on my knees – in volleyball; the Mennonite blonde boy who gave me yellow roses and a jade ring when I graduated and who is a doctor. He tracked me and now telephones out of the blue, thirty years later. "They never get over you," my mother brags. "They never recover from you," she says, now wistful and impressed with what can only be termed an unrepresentative sample. But before, that ability to attract was my dread disease, a threat to – maybe the source of – the family's instability. Nurturer? No, she was a tender, keeping the puck out of the net whenever she could see it coming, sometimes a butterfly flail to keep it out. But remote, elitist, too smart for the rest of the team. My mother survived, but not in a way that could be considered useful to a writer. Time may change my mind.

I like the idea that your father's death is still with you in the essays you write.

—Oh yeah, I haven't written about it sufficiently in a way, because I did write about my mother's death and my mother's life in the eighties. I haven't written about my father's life and my father's death in a way that really puts it to rest for me.

—My father was simple, in the best aesthetic sense of that word and I, too, want to sustain my life with him through art, or maybe to finish our relationship with appropriate closure, the kind only a taut short story provides. But when I try to write about him, he becomes so complex he's pointillist, he's feathers on a Barred Rock: black and white but layered thick. This man was an auctioneer who played tennis and golf and loved les Canadiens, his only outrage a bad call by the linesman: "Ah c'mon fellas!" He loved a good – or bad – pun, women's ankles, "Up a Lazy River" by the Mills Brothers. He anticipated the sports news at eleven o'clock. But he was also once a fair-skinned high school drop-out off to war and then caught and kept in a German POW camp. He once feigned suicide – the newspapers fell for it – just to get away from us, just for awhile. The best thing my father did for me was be like feathers.

In this new collection, the mood is much different, more elegaic. But the prose is different, too. You've always put simple images into complex contexts, but now there seem fewer details, and the context seems simpler. Much less scene-setting choreography as in, say, *The Sportswriter*. Is that because of the themes, or is it just part of your evolution?

—Well, that's how you read them. And so you must be right about the way you read them. But yours is an opinion, nothing more.

—I was going to say you're becoming more Hemingway-esque.

—Oh please, I hope not. That would certainly disappoint me.

—I thought that would make you mad. I said, "I was going to say" it, but I didn't. Don't be mad.

—If I'm not better than Hemingway I should give it up. The world gets complexer and he doesn't. Basically, particularly with those stories of his, as good as they are and affecting as they are, basically the point of view is that of an adolescent.

—You mean Hemingway's point of view?

—Yeah, of a kind of suppressed maturity.

—Hence, his suicide?

—I wouldn't know about that, but probably. Yes, in general suicide – or its repeated and more public attempts – might be seen as the expression of a kind of suppressed maturity.

—You said in an old interview that the inclusion of the opthamologist in the story "Rock Springs" was accidental. The interviewer pushed you to say something about sight and blindness and all that, but you wouldn't. I've found at least two others in the new book. Now, are these more than accidental? What's with all the opthamologists?

—I think it's a word. I just stick the word in a sentence. Whenever I see other words that one likes in a sentence, I'm pleased, I'm happiest, and so I'm not putting them in for anything that has to do with vision, or blindness. Again, you could say moral blindness and you could get a lot of PhD students to agree with you but you wouldn't get the author to agree.

—But you're not making fun of those PhD students?

—Nope.

—When I moved to the country, to a shingled cabin on Becher Bay and a community linked by hayfields and free range eggs, I had been recently released from university and its theories. I read the authentic details of rural experience out my living room window: junco, herring ball, dozer boat, pike pole. I read nature writers – the Transcendentalists; the newsboys turned eco-journo rockstars in primo-tents along any river; Emily Carr and her sad expertise – and I paid attention to their nouns, their connecting tissue. I watched colour lighten in May on the red cedar, and texture convert on browning bracken. I saw birds through a bastard-saw honed vision and heard their tone clusters. I memorized their names. First lambing season, I learned new words for stuck and sick and abortion; I connected stars and colostrom and warm molasses in a midnight poem never voiced: too abstract. I was ready to find words sufficiently germanic and consonant to fit nature's ugly turns, I was going to make the anti-pastoral into something sharp, clean.

But then the nouveau critics down east passed the legislation: Get urban, get punchy. Those days are gone, man, we're all on-line, we are all one big connected city so get with it, grow up, be vegan. Get a tuxedo. Get high heels or just get high. Get a personal trainer and browse the bars. Pick friends with Underwoods and crantinis, or better friends with laptops and craft beers and agents. Get cleavage. Do you know what happens to the septic fields of vegetarians? Are you finding material in the same places you used to? I'm not asking where you find it so don't get mad. Do the same things move you, Richard?

—I'm just takin' notes, you know, I'm just takin' notes all the time. In essence, where I am finding material is in what I hear, what I hear people say, what I think about what people say, what I read in the newspapers, what I see on TV, what I read in other books, yeah, my source material is unending. Things that move me? I think a lot of things move me, so I will assume that the same things do move me, matters of life and death, matters of love disappointed and love realized, relationships between parents and their children, the difficulties of spacial and physical dislocation, the adaptations necessary to new landscape, those kinds of things are the same things that move me.

—Do you still venture up to Saskatchewan to hunt? You seem a frequent visitor to Canada. Is it the hunting and fishing that draws you? Do you still run with Jim Harrison and Thomas McGuane and the boys? Do you fish on the West Coast, was that ever a part of the business?

—Yeah, Ray Carver and I did it for years and when he died I quit going 'cause I don't get along with his wife. Not that she would take me fishing anyway. She might take me out on a boat and throw me in with a big piano tied to my leg, if she possibly could, but I don't, I quit doing that when Ray died. And now I have a house in Maine and I do some. I haven't seen McGuane in a long time, I see Jim once in a while. The odd thing about life as it has gone on, I see fewer and fewer and fewer people of any kind and particularly fewer of my writer colleagues. I'm still friendly with Jim, Jim's very dear to me, and Tom, who I'm less friendly with, we lead different kinds of lives. I don't hunt with either of them. I mostly hunt with my wife.

—Thirty years I was a city chick and came to the country without friends from that botched landscape. I lived in the city when it meant something, before it meant so little. I disagree with you: it is not complexer. Those Eastern pundits want me to believe that urban has not been covered. They seek a new urbanity? These press corps dilettantes have only just discovered the city's gifts – inflated price tag still dangling from its sleeve – and so prescribe that art must cover the action, the family and its flirting, cheating, and corrupt inventories, the flippo drugs for which the privileged brats of my graduating class now hock mumsy's Doulton figurines. Thirty years ago in my Vancouver, kids were snatched from Halloween streets; hanging oneself from a tree in Maple Grove park was optional for teenage boys with meanstreak dads and a sexuality not defined by the push and grunt of a rugby scrum; bleached blonde and bosomy mothers kept mid-mornings open for Mr. Neighbour; drunken writers blew it under the viaduct; incurable diseases – cancer a dirty word that might be catching – were kept secret; gentle men like my father gave up on commerce and its ladder and ran away from home. Now what? What's complexer now?

I looked to the Strait of Juan de Fuca and Race Rocks and Cascadia, to the spawning of sockeye salmon in a desperate and detergent-fouled Goldstream River, not for the consolation of cheapshit metaphor, not for lack of imagination. I know the city's stupid secrets, printed as they are now in a too-sharp digital format. I know the city; I want what came before. Why did we abandon that? Who will read the city's history, trace its underground streams, and where? Treeplanters with poems shoved into their knapsacks? Mention a raven now and bingo: you're a) too pastoral or b) a fucking racist.

Does knowing the *New Yorker* will publish the best of your work change the writing of that work in some way?

—It might, to be honest with you, but I'm not aware of it. There may be some sort of pre-cognitive selection that goes on in the things I will and won't write about which means that they're adapted to what I think the *New Yorker*'s sensibilities are, but the *New Yorker* has a wide sensibility, often an erratically wide sensibility and I don't think that I make any adaptations to fit in. I won't get paid enough money if I publish elsewhere and I don't have a teaching job.

—Wait now. I wouldn't call what I do "job," at least not in the "accrue capital and security and retire well in Irish linen" sense of the word.

—I'm always trying to kind of angle for the bucks here.

—Oh, to have bucks for which to angle! Are you suggesting I am my own victim? That I should quit my so-called job and write cheatin' hurtin' stories for the huge rags? Okay, sign me up. Will I need to learn to live on less, just until the real money starts pouring in? If I buy a second house in the Gulf Islands, should I have someone – a former student or hardluck alco-poet maybe – rent it while I winter in, say, Thessalonika? Do I charge them the going rate, or discount for artists and small press losers? What purpose will landscape serve in my fiction? Why will my men all be sort of western guys? Why will I have trouble writing about women?

—This period in my life in which I've been publishing stories in the *New Yorker*, it won't last forever, it'll go away, other writers will come along and take those slots. It's just been this time for me, this period.

—That drawl, that sonorousness and suggestion of ice clinking in a good glass, you have such a pleasing voice, I hear it always when reading your work, even though I try to dismiss it so I can get a clean reading of a character.

—Before I lock 'em up and put 'em in a book, I read 'em aloud myself, so I know what their essential rhythms are.

—Your writing has never relied on irony for its power.

—Nope.

—Sincerity seems more to the point with your work.

—Yup. I'm an essentialist.

—We are being told that we have reached the end of irony. Does this supposed cultural shift have importance for a writer like you?

—No. No. It has no importance for me and it isn't true. I mean, we haven't reached the end of irony, are you kidding? That's such a cultural myopia that says things like that. Another day will dawn whether we want it to or not. No, I don't think irony is under any attack and all that may be happening to it is that it's being replaced.

—You are the king of the retrospective narrator. You often choose the retrospective voice when sons are recalling fathers, and you achieve a lovely split consciousness, at once young and also painfully wise and old. Why do you choose that perspective?

—I can tell you exactly the cause: I read Sherwood Anderson when I was twenty-three years old, and I was so moved by "Death in the Woods," and I wanted to know why so much that I thought, "oh gee, if I could just write stories like that for the rest of my life, I would." That's the exact reason.

—With Earl in "Rock Springs" you've said it's to prove that he made it out of the life he was living, the mistakes he kept making.

—Yeah, that's right, and the presumption about that kind of a narrative set-up is that somebody has survived it well enough to tell it. And so it is hopeful, perspectively.

—*The Sportswriter's* Frank Bascombe – also a retrospective guy who survives – calls hockey something like "a boring game played by Canadians." I understand Frank, I think, and know the irony implied in a character like him, one who makes his living writing about something he cares little about. Sure, Frank likes baseball and a little basketball, but that's it. He has to write about something he doesn't care about because he's so undone by grief – his little boy's death – that any emotion – real passion or glee or sorrow – will unhinge everything and he'll end up a suicide. So, for him, hockey has to be "a boring game played by Canadians."

Because, you see, Frank will never be a player, never a good body, a salvage king, a hero in Hanna, Alberta. He'll never make it through three playoff rounds and into the NHL finals skating and hip checking and scoring off wrist shots on only one leg, he won't spend the next year coming back from a litany of arthroscopic invasions, throwing the ball around the yard with his little dark-haired girl, Isabella, maybe croquet, his happy winner's face made handsome by three hundred stitches in fifteen years. Or, here. Frank will not almost lose his life mid-season to a rogue cancer and, chemo be damned, come back a threat in the playoffs and pass and score while renegades cross-check and board him and test how well he's stitched together, his blonde Finnish hair just poking through and he looks like a brushcut kid just trying out. Or, here. Frank will never get cut loose from long-term drug rehab to compete – compete in the sexiest and most primal way – in the Olympics because his nation wants him – We forgive you! – on the ice. No. Frank is too busy. Too busy hunting stupid sex, his grief pushed back and up, back and up, back and up. Frank is too afraid of commitment – way fucked up, in other words – to appreciate the game of Canadian hockey.

—Hold on.

—No, that's just the rooster.

—Hold on. There's someone at the door. *Hello? No, I don't need them, just leave them outside the door. What? No, darlin', I'm on the bed right now, so I don't want you to make it. No. I'm* liein' *on the bed and* talkin' *on the phone. Thank-you.*

—You wouldn't be naked would ya, Richard?

—I would be, but I happen not to be. That's what Scott says, he said, "Now when you talk to her you can sort of lie back on the bed," and I said, "Oh, is she coming to the room?"

—That's funny. Speaking of infidelity, it's obviously a pattern in your work. That was a good segué don't you think?

—Pretty good. We'll see.

—I'm wondering if your writing treats faithfulness now with cynicism.

—No, it doesn't. No, look.

—You're mad again.

—Look. I'll tell you something. I don't feel that way. And I think one of the things I learned as I looked through this collection, as I was putting it together in essence, kind of going through it last spring, and seeing what fit together where and what was like something else and if anything needed to be nicked out of the slick because it repeated something, one of the things I noted was how much the stories, albeit in an unanticipated way, credit the virtues of family. In a story where the greatest source of solace for the woman is her mother, and even in a story where this sort of creepy guy kind of blunders into the family, the family still, even though the wife has been expunged, the family – which is to say the father and his daughter – is still a kind of image of integrity and hope. So, no. I think you could find other images, too, which say that what these people in these stories are playing along the edge of is not the dissolution of family, the dissolution of marriage and fidelity, at all.

—I read your stories with eighteen-year-olds, one story per term, and I'm gladdened by their response. These are slim boys who have yet to work the green chain. They made the swim team and went to the finals in Kelowna. Their dads and moms are teacher/homemakers. The dog is a retriever and older sister, Sarah, is in South Africa on a Rotary exchange. Maybe they know a girl with an eating disorder, a friend split apart by a drunk driver. They keep away from the kid in the dorm who went professional and made the Vancouver Ravens lacrosse team.

—Thank-you for doing that.

—For many, it is their first exposure to random sex and petty larceny and Mercedes ragtops the colour of fruit and guys like Earl or Frank in fiction, and they seem to think, Hey, I never knew it was okay to write about that stuff!

—Young readers can definitely get some news in short stories.

—What needs to happen before readers take to the short story as easily as they do to novels?

—I don't really understand that. I really don't know.

—Is it too precious a form? Do all the rules and regulations scare readers into thinking they must find a cut jewel and stick it on their finger? Or did Alice make writers go too pastoral or domestic and write only about lonely women and their unfortunate choices? Do you favour the urban edge *vis à vis* short fiction?

—I don't understand why readers don't read short stories with a great deal more alacrity than they do. I don't get it. It's just something culturally that I don't get. Every time I even try to hazard a guess about that my sense of conviction runs out from under me. I don't know.

—This time last year, every male writer I know had an anecdote about partying with Candace Bushnell. Do you have such a story? Last year, men on either side of the country, on the same weekend, were e-mailing me about having partied with Candace Bushnell.

—Shame on them. What an indiscrete thing to do.

—Talk about it?

—Put it on the e-mail.

—That's what we've come to.

—Well, so to speak, I guess it is. I have no recollection of Ms. Bushnell, though I'm sure she's a very nice person. I'd like to meet her.

—Do you have anxieties about writing in the first person from the narrative perspective of a guy who has sex with eighteen women after his little boy dies, or a guy who thinks Canadians and their sport are boring? Are you afraid friends and family might confuse author and character?

—Absolutely not.

—Is that maturity, or did you never have those anxieties?

—I don't give a shit.

—And did you never give a shit?

—If I did I made myself quit.

—One more question, Richard, then my time's up. Who's writing better short stories than you are?

—Well let's see. Uh, Alice. Alice certainly. Yes, Alice.

—Does Faulkner still have no equal?

—Faulkner wasn't a real good story writer, he wasn't a real master of that form. Carver wrote better stories than I do. I generally don't feel competitive with other writers. I know lots of writers who write really well and when I see them writing really well, I don't often think to myself, "they're better than I am."

—So, you're not competitive?

—And I never think to myself, "I'm better than they are." Updike is probably a better sentence maker than I am, but I don't think he writes about as interesting a set of things as other people, including myself.

—But you're not competitive.

—He's such a lapidary master of making sentences, I think sometimes that can be a delimiter of what he is able to take in. Mavis Gallant, probably, writes better stories than I do. With Alice, there's just no use. She just is a better story writer than I am and is better at it, and I'm sorry she is, actually, I wish I were as good as she is but I'm just not.

—Thank-you for taking the time for this.

—Well, thank-you. It's been a pleasure. Now, will I be seeing you in Vancouver next week?

—Oh. I'm not sure. I live on Vancouver Island. I left Vancouver, you'll remember, and I rarely get back. Occasional upscale hair cuts. I might be there, yes. I could be.

—Then you'll come up and say hello if you are, won't you?

—I will say hello.

—Do that.

—I will.

—Good.

—I'm grateful, Richard.

—Me, too.

I Flirt with JANET JONES-GRETZKY

—Your hands are bigger than Wayne's.

—Oh my gosh, you noticed that? Don't say I'm taller, just don't. He hates that. Wayne has a great deal of pride and he's extremely competitive. He doesn't like to lose, even to me. I'm going to pour more water on the rocks. I like it very hot. Cute bracelet you're wearing; my daughter makes those for her friends.

—What's that smell?

—I've added several drops of eucalyptus special for saunas. We find it really soothes muscles after a workout and it clears Wayne's sinuses. Sometimes, we add sandalwood, and the kids like a lemon milk we get from Australia. They say it smells like Easter, but we don't see the connection.

—You've done remarkable designing in here. The cedar actually seems more Louis XV than Finnish.

—Oh my gosh, that's what Jarri Kurri says when he visits! "Yawnet" – that's what he calls me! – "Yawnet, what have you done to my country here? What's about the arches and the swirls? What's about the cherubs?" he always says, and I'm, "Jarri, please, relax, it's my style!" He's a lovely, lovely person.

—You like athletes.

—I love athletes. And dancers. People who take their bodies to the limit. But athletes especially. Oops. Sorry. No no. Your leg's fine there, I'll just scootch over a bit. You have very plump calves, very nice. You must work out. How old are you, if you don't mind the question?

—You were engaged for three years to Vitas Gerulaitis, the Lithuanian Lion. Long wavy blonde hair before stars were allowed to, an enormous twinkle. Only six feet tall, but he appeared much longer. In the late seventies, I watched tennis in Vancouver. Because I lived only blocks away and

65

adored his company, I lunched with my father at the Vancouver Lawn Tennis club once a week. My dad was a great player, adored Arthur Ashe and Rod Laver but didn't go for the new style of athlete, those who earned millions but couldn't behave on the court or off it. I was living with my first serious love, a guitar player from Wawa, Ontario. He, too, was Lithuanian and I teased him with Vitas. My boyfriend's hair was bad brown, short and already thinning. His skin was not tanned and smooth, but pale and deeply pocked from neck to forehead. Though his eyes were blue, the glasses he wore were so thick you couldn't tell. He had a habit of squeezing his crotch in conversation, didn't matter who he was talking to. He wore country music shirts. My favourite was a gingham pearl button number he had worn the afternoon his father shot himself in the basement in Wawa.

—Vitas was a lovely, lovely man.

—And also a man with addictions, treated for cocaine indulgence, notorious for his back-to-back women. Dead too young from inhaling carbon monoxide a pool heater leached into the room where he slept. My boyfriend only went stupid on a glass of cheap scotch. He liked cigarettes but they thrashed his voice and he longed to have the clear high notes of Glen Campbell or the Everly Brothers or the Beach Boys. As for women, who knows? When a guy plays the bars and stays out late and has a sense of humour bordering on infantile, when he's a great bass player and moves on stage in a contorted, amoebic, quasi-Joe Cocker way, women go nuts, go figure. I had an imagination. My self-esteem had a poor plus-minus. Lonely. In bed at night waiting, I made up stories – he was the star – and there was always another woman: prettier, more confident and more talented than me. In my twenties, I wanted a man to worship me in a subtle, sophisticated way. I imagined a relationship where I was the implied queen, and my boyfriend would thrill to see me, would miss me like crazy, would realize how incredibly lucky he was to have a chick like me: talented, smart, funny and lovely, with the right ratio of sexuality to domesticity. Don't all women covet this worship?

—Vitas didn't mean to hurt me and I'm sure your boyfriend didn't know you were so sad. He sounds very sweet. Were you getting much exercise at the time?

—This was two years after knee surgery and a time of inept rehab. So, no. I couldn't walk in even a kitten heel. I swam lengths at the club, but drank beer to reward my get up and go. And wine. I thought booze would make me more fun to be with, but I had begun a nine-year phase of misery notorious for dawn-to-dawn sipping and much weepiness. I'd pick music – Emmylou and Roseanne Cash – that would press me further down. "Quit using that music to get depressed," he'd shout. "They're not talking about you." I was not the queen. I was ignored and resented, and my dog lived with my parents, for chrissakes. How could I be happy? Now at one time, you folks had four dachshunds.

—Oh my gosh, you know everything! Yes. We had three when Wayne was traded to New York and we left those here in California. The kids were so sad, so I really understand your point about not having a dog. Paulina was only eight and she'd cry for the dogs in bed at night. She blamed Wayne. It was hard on him. Those were difficult times, all of us in a penthouse apartment. New York! The light there is so different. But people were very kind to us and we could walk the kids to piano lessons. When we came back here to California, after Wayne's retirement, we built a new house in the hills and had dogs again. That scar on your knee would improve if you rubbed coco butter on it every night. I'll give you a jar before you go. All the players use it. You have pretty knees.

—They sit up too high. That's why the sub-luxing.

—Let's be positive: they're pretty. Perrier? Not too hot for you? This guy you loved didn't work out, huh?

—He eventually had enough of the sadness, the suspicions, how I doubted my own talent.

—Men really really hate doubts.

—He dumped me and found a plain girl from a smaller town, a girl who did more drugs, had a better job, and didn't aspire to be a musician, to be anything. I hooked up with a series of guitar players, same pattern.

—Wow! Very Hollywood!

—But it wasn't, Janet. Here where you live, it's high gloss and everyone looks great and appears to care little about the deeper emotions. Here, people seem small-minded but thoroughly satisfied to be that way, determined to be that way. The doubts expressed here seem more nervous, tic, chattery. And when the lights go out, folks drift into a dreamy sleep with hope for tomorrow's phonecalls and gigs. The doubts I had were life-threatening. There was no gloss and that upset me. The deeper emotions I felt, the untouchable wants and faithless love and regrets that I believed good, enduring music would come from were ignored or mocked by bar musicians. Have a drink, they said, turn up the treble, and so I did and the pain got loud, shrill and ugly or went deeper and made a hole in my gut. It's getting harder to breathe in here, but I like it.

—I don't think you're right about people in California. Turn around. I want to rub your shoulders. How did they get up so high? Relax a little. Let me slide my leg along there. Oops, sorry. They get in the way after five kids! Wayne and I have a pretty normal life, you know. We support each other. Hockey comes first for him. Actually, he says it comes first, second, third, and I come fourth! Ha!

—You think that's funny?

—Oh, sure.

—Really?

—Oh, sure. That's Wayne. He's always been very focussed.

—You said when you were twenty-seven and marrying him that you might want two children. Here you are in your forties. You have a girl of fourteen and a toddler of two and three boys between them. Your work is domesticity and public relations. You cheer for Canadian teams. You sit a row behind Wayne and his staff at gold medal games and he does remember to hug and kiss you when they win, but only after he does it with Kevin Lowe, and then a couple of seconds late for my taste. He claims to value family. He's delighted to have so many kids and worships his parents. And yet. Given the opportunity to coach a team in Arizona – California and Arizona look close on the map, but flights between LA and Phoenix are what? Five, six, seven hours? –

—We also have a home in Scottsdale. It's not so bad.

—He told us all that he had to weigh his options: more time with family versus more time with hockey. This is a guy who's been playing since he was two, Janet. Hasn't he had enough time with the game?

—Oh, Wayne could never be without hockey.

—You're missing my point.

—What's this? I'm not going to press too hard there.

—Bone spur. Apparently I damaged my neck as a kid but I don't remember when or how.

—Does this cause you pain?

—Not right now, but it does. If I knit too long, or sleep on a bad pillow.

—You knit?! Oh, I wish I did. You are a remarkable woman.

—So he tells the world he has to think it over: Family. Game. Family. Game. And then bingo: he's decided. All the sports broadcasters, those who know him as Gretz and pretend the buddy-buddy bit, predict he will announce his intention to become coach. So even the fat and flatulent hockey writers know he's going to pick the game over his family. And then there's you saying it will be nice for your kids to see him doing what so much of his life was all about. Please.

—Yes.

—A man to whom you've given five children, your acting career, your name, your youth and your womanhood, your whole self, really. In his autobiography, he promised to return the favour of your sacrifice. When? Time's almost up! A guy who caroused with the best of them in the Oilers caligulaic phase, the Playboy bunnies, the celeb tennis tourneys and post-game hot tubs, and whose most admirable quality, everyone concurs, is that he hates to lose. To some of us, that's not an admirable quality, Janet. It's not heroic: it's childish and selfish.

—Yes.

—I watched him after that first game he coached against the Canucks. Each time the camera caught him, it seemed he was struggling with indigestion. After the game, he looked exhausted: his face was lined, his eyes blank and dull and mesmerized by what he'd just seen. He was clearly still having trouble with his stomach. I know his father had terrible ulcers; I'm wondering why this man would choose to re-embrace the dawn-to-dawn stomach acid, the weight of the hockey world on his shoulders, the banality of the twice-daily press conference, and not spend all his time being around gorgeous you and your gorgeous kids. It's time to be the queen.

—Yes, but I've always been that. Wayne's always made me feel that way. We're very close and it doesn't take a 24/7 living arrangement to prove our love and his devotion to me and the kids. Even the queen likes to have time to herself.

—Guys don't play for two teams at the same time.

—He's not playing; he's coaching. And coaching's kind of what it's like to be a parent. So he's coaching two teams, and I think that's just lovely. If anyone can make it work, Wayne can. Your shoulders would be much lower if you didn't get so serious about things. And that would make your neck appear longer.

—Do you and Wayne ever dance when you go out?

—Ha!

—What?

—You're kidding?

—No. You've always been a dancer. You appear to dance even when you walk. Your limbs are long and lithe, even your fingers are astonishing. Did you land a guy who would dance with you?

—Hockey players don't dance.

—What about in the kitchen? Do you ever get into your jammies and, late at night, kids asleep, do a few twirls in each other's arms around that oak island, you singing softly into his ear and him holding you close at the waist? God, you'd look gorgeous, the two of you.

—Maybe when we were younger and coming in from a party. People in Canada shouldn't worry so much. I think we've proved that we're pretty solid as far as being a loving family and the love we have for each other. We make sure we have a good time.

—Regrets?

—None really. Except my husband and I wish we'd both been able to attend college.

—Or university.

—Yes. We've tried to give our kids one thing over everything: a good education. Both Wayne and me were working so young, on the road, and high school was not a priority and we know we missed out. All our kids speak more than one language and their studies come first.

That's just the right heat now, don't you think? Imagine all the poison coming out through those pores. Let the poison go.

—Does Paulina have a tutor when she's on the road modeling and singing and dancing?

—No, but she doesn't do a lot of that. We just want her to have every opportunity if something comes up. We want her to be prepared to excel.

—You could still go to school, you know.

—Ha!

—I ended that string of guitar players with a clean cut: no more music, no more booze, no more Vancouver. With a few thousand dollars from my grandmother, I returned to university at thirty years old. I stumbled at first, tried to find a man too soon and lost concentration. Time management was a challenge. Then I went quiet and close and studious. Alone in my white apartment, the hardwood floors, some Dutch-Indonesian waitressing on weekends. I fell in love with my brain again. I read Chaucer out loud with the wonky swerves of Middle English, and wrote short stories on my little couch with the bright coastal light singing through the big windows. I read four novels a week just to keep up and made hearty soups every weekend. University was a safe place to reinvent myself. They give nice grades for hard work. All the people there are not just like you and your friends and so your life takes on a different sort of colour, maybe not so bright but more appealing. Plenty of people older than I was had gone back to school with the same pleasure in mind: listen to smart people talk. You like athletes because they push their bodies to the limit; you could push your brain and get the same thrill.

—I think it's too late for me. Five kids!

—William Kittredge, travelling Arizona, wrote, "find the good books, not just the guidebooks . . . read them, mark them up, use them as tools, carry them with you. No place can be real emotionally unless we've imagined life there, and our imagining is not likely to be very substantive if not informed." Read the books, Janet. Take a course on the peoples who lived in Phoenix thousands of years before the first blondes arrived, who prayed hard not for a clearcut breakaway in overtime, but for rain. Some believed they became clouds at death and brought rain to their people as a reward for life lived and lost. Help them resist the white man's dams. Forget the handicapped kids; do good for a civilization on the downslide. You're near the Salt River where the Pima people believe they descended from the Hohokam, 300BC. They farmed and built canal irrigation systems throughout the valley, a system still in use. Imagine. The Pima are ingenious basketmakers, too. Willow shoots, cattails, and devil's claws are split, trimmed and shaved to just the right thickness. In the shadow of Red Mountain, twelve thousand acres are under cultivation – cotton, melons, onions, potatoes. Life is a maze, the Pima believe, a search for balance – physical, social, mental and spiritual. In the middle of the maze are found a person's dreams. The Sun God is waiting there to bless us and let us die. This maze isn't all about finding the way out; it's about finding the way in. You reach your dream at the middle of the maze. Life is a maze, Janet. It's a puzzle to respect, happy or sad.

—You must miss the music.

—Why is it, do you think, that athletes would never choose a woman like me and always go for someone like you. What's the difference between you and me?

—How does that feel? Turn around, look at me now: the only difference I can see is that I'm maybe a bit more positive than you are. I've learned to always see the good, to always trust that good things will happen and that I can handle any situation. And I never dwell on what's gone wrong, whether it's one of the kids being late for a piano lesson or a loss in an important tournament. Hockey players will teach you this: always look forward to the next game, never dwell on the mistakes of the last one, don't even think about that shot you missed or the check that blew by you. Look ahead. We teach our kids this. You can learn, too.

—You don't think we're different in other ways? Is your waist still twenty-two inches?

—Listen. You don't seem like a girl who's interested in surfaces, in the superficial. So why should it matter that I look like this and you enjoy a different beauty? You loved that boyfriend of yours, the Lithuanian, despite his flaws. You had a connection that was based, maybe, on something other than surface beauty. You're a very pretty woman. You should make the most of that and never doubt that men notice you. You might want to rewrap the towel now. My husband's going to come and get us when he's in from the airport and we can all have a glass of wine by the pool. Let me tuck it: there. Stunning. This colour blue is wonderful against your skin and hair. And see what that extra tuck does for your curves? See?

I Flirt with MICHAEL ONDAATJE

—You look like that border collie, the one rounding the curve, fancy scarf.

—That's an Aussie Shepherd.

—Pardon?

—Oz. Ee. Shep. Erd.

—Right, sorry, I should've known that.

—You mean what with all the grey in all this hair, the shaggy beard, my white-blue eyes?

—And the work ethic. The intensity. The constant editing. You make us all want to write, you know. I'm having trouble understanding you, Mr. Ondaatje. Maybe turn my way just a little and try not to speak into the wind. The grass feels damp but we get a good view of the ring from down here, down at pooch level. Say: if you were a dog, what breed would you be?

—These are working breeds and I've always preferred spaniels or hounds. A more reclining breed, less busy. Fragrant paws but the ability to lick them clean and then fall asleep. I must say the idea of bestowing a prize on a dog – on anything, especially writers – doesn't sit well with me. Still, the Aussie Shepherd looks pleased with his ribbon. Or is it the biscuit? Or is it cos of the attention from his master, though I don't much like the length of her skirt for an outdoor event this time of year? Or does he know we're all watching and now admire him? I do like this part, when they parade, and the winner grins and looks so immensely pleased.

—Spaniels for me, too. A liver and white springer as a child and then, the year after my sister died when I turned sixteen, another springer which I named Thurber.

—Nice. A hint of the highbrow and comic.

—You once had a spaniel named Flirt, didn't you?

75

—My personal life, my past personal life, my present one: these I won't discuss, even with a dog lover like you.

—I was sixteen and gone dumb from the death of my sister, and Thurber was a gift from my sad parents, a way to keep me in the world with a soft hairy neck to weep on. I bussed tables that summer in Stanley Park, a thousand acres, where my sister had worked, and I bagged leftover bread crusts at night and came early the next morning and fed the ducks and swans at Lost Lagoon before my shift. I was sixteen and dumbed by loss. My hair was long and straight and I didn't wear make-up. I listened to James Taylor and loved Glen Campbell, even then, the variety of his licks, both vocal and instrumental, the new poetry of John Hartford and Jimmy Webb, words we hadn't heard before and the finger-picking, the bluegrass laid over pop psychadelic in its own way.

—Yes, Webb's poetry. But not the "someone left the cake out in the rain."

—I read books about the American civil rights movement, especially keen on Bobby Seale and the Black Panthers and wanted to Seize the Time but not sure why, given where and how I lived. And a woman I babysat for gave me *The Female Eunuch* and I read that, too. At the job in evergreened Stanley Park, I was stupid with grief and with a new morality that said a) take what you want and b) anyone can and will die. My boss, a twenty-nine-year-old married man, fell for me.

—Ah.

—You've known the same heart-scandal, the illogic of emotion that can make those numbers add up, the sado-masochism of illicit romance.

—Huh?

—Infidelity. You were a teenager lured and loved by an adult. You were nineteen; she was thirty-four and married. Sure you were Oxford-educated and serious and matured by dislocation, but you were a teenager.

—I've never cared for the sameness of these Scottish Terriers. This could get boring.

—Maybe no smoking here.

—I'll just hold onto it. That guy's sure proud of his tight little shorts at this time of year.

—I remember not much about the affair, except his sailboat moored at False Creek, his golden retrievers – Sally and Sarah – his funky green, bulbous fendered Ford pickup, a dog show we attended in Seattle, and his kindness. I remember the day I attended a school-sponsored screening at the Ridge Theatre of Franco Zeffirelli's "Romeo and Juliet" –

—The best version really. 1968. Shot on location in Italy and so the lighting is gorgeous, like plums and honey. Sixteen-year-old Olivia Hussey as Juliet. The cinematography won an Oscar. The costumes, my god. The brilliant bit of nudity on the after-marriage morning. Very sixties counter-culture romantic. What a film. I'd like to see it again, maybe this afternoon. Think about it.

—I saw the movie on a west coast wet and grey afternoon and was moved by the double suicide since I was already beginning to understand the kiss of escape and death's happy alternative. My manfriend picked me up at the theatre in his dog-stink truck and chose that time to say our relationship – it had been a year – was off. His wife wanted him back now. He drove me home and dropped me off.

—Uh-oh. That movie was good enough that you'd have a hard time separating yourself from it cos it would be like your life was the movie's next scene, or a replay of previous scenes. And what with your long dark hair, I'll bet you did some identifying with Juliet's beauty and predicament.

—That night, I swallowed a bottle of 222s, thinking that simply by willing myself to die, an inept medicine would be transformed into lethal. "All suicides all acts of privacy are romantic" as your own Webb says in *Coming Through Slaughter. It's still a good idea*, writes another. I took to bed and played Jim Croce's Greatest Hits over and over on the big turntable in my dead sister's room.

—I knew it. "Time in a Bottle?"

—I preferred the up-tempo even while bereft. Leroy Brown.

—Your parents?

—Not home or not present. During the evening, Thurber barked and fretted at the front door and I floated filmically downstairs to settle her. I looked out through the sidelight windows and there on the lit porch sat a gorgeous golden cocker spaniel, wet and whimpering. I opened the big door. "Go home," I said, stern and drugged, "Go. Home." and closed the door and went back up to bed's final frontier, to the south side of Chicago. An hour passed, I went back down – clearly the stupid meds were not working – and opened the door again. The lovely dog shot past my legs into the hallway and folded down onto my mother's favourite turquoise Indian rug, exhausted. Thurber did, too.

—A ghost.

—Exactly. That's what I thought. So I took this dog as a sign that I was meant to carry on. That there were beings in the world that wanted my care. *We who have considered suicide take our daily walk/with death and are not lonely.* Again, a Webb.

—There's no better smell: wet spaniel on a hard night.

—Those kilts; I like how they flip up around the turns and show a bit of hamstring. But they seem redundant next to all the Scottie dogs.

—And the Fair Isle sweaters. Certainly not flattering to the mature bosom.

—If you want another cup of coffee, Michael, you say so. I can go for it if you'd rather not get up, but no more doughnuts for you, mister. Twenty minutes a day on the stationary bike would do wonders for that waist. The jowls are more bull mastiff than hyperthin sheepdog.

Some critics have explored the relationship between creativity and the death instinct in your work. Why, they ask, is the artist sometimes a killer, sometimes a suicide. They want to resolve the ambiguous nature of creativity in your work.

—Look over there: Jesus, that's not a dog, that's someone's failed poem about a dog. Where are the legs? The neck? Look here: I've said that the problems Buddy Bolden has – you're wondering most about him, right? – are the problems any artist has at some time. Uh-oh. The pretty redhead's lost the beat with her pup; she's right to pull out of the parade.

—How to escape art? How to be both creativity's slave and its master? Whether to choose madness as a way to restore order in the chaos of art?

—Well, yeah, okay. And how an artist strives for originality – innovation – and meaningful work in a society that values formulaic cover-singing, embellishment-heavy American Idols chosen over the phone by the screen-loving masses.

—Whatever happened to a simple melody? *Just sing it straight,* my Lithuanian boyfriend used to gripe. *More hot licks than a teenage nymphomaniac,* he'd say.

—How does a musician like Bolden, a man like him and with his appetites and the radical conversation he has with his mouth and music, with his hands and body, how does a player like Bolden survive in a time and place and landscape that rejects chaos and the improvisation that is its antidote. Art's consumers are all about plot, you see, and Bolden was not able to connect the dots. Fame has a high cost.

—Improv is anecdote?

—Ant. i. Dote.

—Tell me about Buddy Bolden. Describe his body, for example.

—You've read the book.

—Many times, and I've looked often at the band photo on the cover. So long and narrow, his hands fastidious on the horn even when posed. The smile: is that arrogance or flirting? He looks so great, so lean in those clothes.

—I . . .

—He is so erotic in the book, so unable to control passions. Both in love with women and contemptuous of them. In love with jazz and scornful of others who love it but want control. Wild about the street and also its victim. Able to disappear into sex and music but so powerless that both swallow him and refuse to spit him out. He is digested. So willing to be naked. So silent yet in love with words. I'd like to run my tongue over his abs, then his wrist.

—I . . .

—His conflict between form and shapelessness. His fragility and yet sinewy strength, like cat gut, or baling twine. He played the devil's music and hymns at the same time, he didn't choose: he merged them because, well, of course. And his falls into madness are erotic, linked to women and music's siren, a pushing of the body and mind past their frontiers and finally a long, high note of surrender and a crossing over into the dark, the silence forever.

—I . . .

—You?

—I . . . Listen. You shouldn't see the book as a prototype for your own relationships to art or to men or to the street. Cos it's not wise to have a crush on Buddy Bolden. Surely you deserve better, more tenderness, kinder men less concerned with their own reputation. A woman who loves the smell of a wet spaniel is entitled to romance that is not superficial or self-serving.

—Actually . . . here: my notes say it's you who loves the smell of a wet spaniel. My next suicide was landscape-induced. I left the city and headed up to a watery world and a long shoreline, to a husband, to musicians on the lam and living on boats at the breakwater. Thurber came, too, but would not venture to the beach across the road, would not slip her paws into the cold and whale-rich Johnstone Strait. The homesteading otters frightened her. When my new and short-term husband was home, she would quaver in her basket by the door. When he wasn't, she would climb onto my lap, though she was too large to do so. I was nineteen and when new husband sailed to fish up north, I again fell for an older, more married man.

—Well, the seventies allowed for this.

—You think? I don't. Betrayal is always about contravention, sadism, adolescence, carelessness. It's always ugly and cowardly. The misery of others is never fine.

—You were a teenager.

—This time it was James Taylor on the turntable.

—Which?

—"Your Smiling Face."

—Irony?

—Yup. And then the pills, champagne, turpentine and the scalpel on my wrists, the back of my hands, any visible vein but never quite deep enough. See?

—Still, you have lovely hands. Working hands. Those are old scars now and the story they tell has moved aside for other, more unpredictable ones. I see the story of a garden in those hands, maybe the hint of guitar chords.

—I was flown to a psychiatric ward down-island and told by the mayor who was also the doctor to stay put until I could be more service to the community. He may have meant this kindly. I took my guitar. I fell there, too, this time for a shrubby yet handsome older alcoholic from Port Alice who claimed he was there because his wife, when she didn't find satisfaction with him, enjoyed an intimate relationship on the kitchen floor with their willing German shepherd. I kissed that man on the beach, truant from my room, the ward. The nurses were fed up with me. My doctor said, *of course. It's all about your father leaving you.* More James Taylor in the afternoon as I began to come around to pleasantness: "Shower the People." Some difficult chords. And soon, back to the city, to a band, the bars, the road.

I can't begin to tell you about my relationship with music and how it broke my heart. I believed I could be original, an innovator and instead played the Eagles and Creedence Clearwater Revival in every dive joint from Port Moody to Prince George for the better part of a decade. In my head, I heard the tone clusters and eight part chords of Benjamin Britten, I heard his *War Requiem* and da Vittoria's clean melodies and gradual harmonies and wanted their complexity in the verse, chorus, verse, chorus, bridge, verse, chorus of country music. Emmylou showed promise, but I was in the bars. My voice a broken record. The crowd an empty glass. My hands too small and inept on the night's high strings.

—You drank.

—I did.

—Christ, who wouldn't?

—And then that music died and me, too, just about. But it wasn't jazz and I wasn't a miracle so no one thought much about the misery of it: the music gone, Thurber left to live in another landscape, the men all old and stoned and hot for the next chick singer. It wasn't jazz. It was tawdry and simplistic country, no room for improv's antidote, no need for it really. So no one cared when I lost it and gave up.

—Yeah, but here you are, what? Twenty years later? And you have a dog?

—Yes.

—And?

—I have a dog, yes.

—And?

—The dog was his dog.

—His?

—Yes. The most recent, the fifteen-year *his*. The dog was his and then he found another woman – younger, happier, better breed, no art – and now it's my dog, our daughter's dog. He came to me and said, "I'm in a relationship with her. I want out."

—Like a dog at the door.

—Yes, desperate to piss or for the ecstasy of chasing squirrels, maybe both.

—Well. *What are we whole or beautiful or good for but to be absolutely broken?* to quote that wisest Webb. You'll be whole again, maybe even broken if you're lucky.

—Our daughter plays horn, you see, trumpet. And her mouth is full of it, her hands automatic in their lust for her instrument. I see her smirk on stage as she flaunts the fedora and the rhythm and its partnering blues. I love that look. She goes to the bright side of the road and then hurtles back to the dark end of our street. Charlie Parker floats down the stairs from her room. His dog trembles with the sound of music. A dachshund.

—Like E.B White.

—Like Wayne Gretzky.

—Still, a hound.

—More terrier than hound. Separation anxiety, no road sense, angry at new lambs, dominant and hard on the cat. She tunnels under the covers at night and I wake with heat against the small of my back and believe he's still beside me, silent as our last years together. At night I dream of Buddy Bolden's form, his mouth. The weight of a hockey player's kind hand on my wrist. My father laughing at a cocktail party and saying, "I'm back." I dream of happy young men with scarred jaws and eyes who desire older women in the new sexual order and I wonder what it was about your first wife – you were nineteen and she was thirty-four – that drew you into her arms and kept you there for so long.

—Great. The sporting breeds. The Irish setter looks tough to beat. Let's stay for one more round. I'd like to see a film this afternoon. You can drop me downtown and I'll find something.

—Are you cold, Mr. Ondaatje, or is it just me?

I Flirt with BENJAMIN BRITTEN

—That's the Pacific Ocean you can smell this evening. Will you stay in the wheelchair, Benjamin, or should we arrange a blanket and pillows on the grass?

—Here will do nicely, in the lovely shade of your purple beech. You really do have some British aesthetics, my dear, at least in this garden. Still, I sense a certain toughness, a recent loss of innocence, reflected in the wildness of the field beyond the fence. Barbed wire next to boxwood, you see. Or perhaps I'm responding to the Canadian sensibility.

—Your mother's last name was Hockey.

—Indeed. Edith Hockey. My mother was never a professional singer, only a keen amateur one with a sweet voice. I miss my mother.

—You visited Canada once in the seventies and called it an extraordinary place and said North America was the locale of the future. Is it?

—Certainly one was worried by a lack of culture, but back then there was terrific energy and vitality in the place. I seriously considered staying over here permanently. But that was eastern Canada. This place, your place is different. Lush and alive in a complex, natural way. When I was a child in England, our nanny would take us on walks to see how many more houses had fallen off the cliff in the next village. If it were too wet for a walk, we'd watch from the nursery window as a tug pulled a fleet of fishing smacks out to sea. Your home reminds me of there, of that. Across the field, would those be Douglas fir, right on your property?

—Fir, yes. Western red cedar. There's a scraggy balsam back there, and vine maples. Indian plum, salmonberries. So lush it drives me crazy; I dream the forest creeping nearer and taking my house. And earthquakes sending trees onto my head.

—Those are fertile dreams, indeed, but they have little to do with trees, I can tell you that. Dreams are the artist's workshop.

—While you were in eastern Canada and thinking of staying, I was in high school in Vancouver and discovering how you could save my heart from breaking. My sister was dead, my parents were dark, I'd quit the volleyball team and grown bored with Grade 11 biology, with analyzing John Donne's sonnets for symbols, with Christian boyfriends and married ones and the ones who played rugby like church. I was thin and tired, and the music of James Taylor or Glen Campbell or Gordon Lightfoot no longer seemed adequate to express my obsessions. Nice chords, some pretty lyrics, nuanced finger-picking, helpful clichés, but something missing in a pop song.

—A teenager likely requires bitonality – the harmonizing of two common chords simultaneously – to express the natural way of being young in a cruel world. Popular music cannot tolerate dissonance, it's a pity but true. Were you at all suicidal? Of course you were, my dear girl, look at those lovely hands of yours. I myself loathed that abominable hole of artistic self-doubt – if you are original, well you are considered a lunatic and consequently become unpopular – but suicide is so cowardly, running away's as bad. I decided I simply had got to stick it out. Wystan once wrote to me this: "If you are really to develop to your full stature, you will have, I think, to suffer and make others suffer, in ways which are totally strange to you at present, and against every conscious value that you have." That is such uplifting advice, I think. But that was Wystan, the dear soul. Between the ages of thirteen and sixteen I knew every note of Beethoven and Brahms.

—That's it. Adolescence is bitonality. Melisma. The enharmonic change. Our choirs were good, our director a genius and demanding. And in the clusters and scaffolds of your difficult and stunning notes required to push, say, *A Ceremony of Carols* to its purest form, I felt my brain and body come together for the first time. I entered a private and turgid room at the core of myself. Beauty. We made records, we festivalled. And at the end of high school, we travelled Europe to sing in churches and schools and to see where all of this beauty came from. And on day two we visited Aldeburgh where you were said to be ill – a return of the heart problems, the murmur from three months old – and we were young, Benjamin, but I knew what it meant to be near you and to express my thanks for all those notes, all that harmony with a million overtones that had saved me from myself. And we stayed in Stuttgart during the World Cup and Germany won that year, 1974, and the streets weren't safe for teenagers from Canada. And we sang, one evening, in Matthew Church in Stuttgart, a town my father bombed in WWII just before Berlin and his own private and turgid room as a young man shot down and imprisoned. And a reporter wrote this about our performance:

"The entire program with several very difficult compositions was presented from memory. The mixed choir sang first. The capacity to invest each respective style with the appropriate feeling was astonishing: delicate in sound and vitally inspired by the director. The girls' choir impressively took up the second half, finishing with the crowning glory – 'Missa Brevis in D' of Benjamin Britten, ravishingly negotiated."

—The Germans said this? Oh, well done. Well done, indeed, my dear. Is that a varied thrush I hear?

—Varied thrush.

—Sounds like a harpsichord.

—It was well done, and we were all so moved during that performance. We could feel it in our bodies, in our hearts. The church was dark and the soccer games were done, most of us had throat infections and homesickness, and we'd lunched in a German village that was mourning the loss of a local farmer's son: his motorcycle crashed on cobbled streets. Sometime during that evening performance – during some bitonal moment – the whole lot of us grew up and into ourselves, into our voices, and became selves. Through your notes. Surely no other composer can say he did this for young people. You knew what you were giving to us, didn't you? You intended it that way.

—Oh, what's this now!!

—Greta.

—Greta?! You have a dachshund named Greta?! Oh Oh Oh!

—She'll get down if you want. She's really my ex-husband's dog and she's not well-trained.

—Oh Oh Oh!

—She shouldn't do that. No kissy! Ask her to get down.

—Not at all. Gilda was ours, Peter's and mine. And another tiny one called Clytie. Your husband was homosexual I gather?

—No, Benjamin. He just loved the breed.

—But where had he encountered the breed?

—I don't know. Not with me.

—No, you seem like spaniels.

—Yes, I had springers.

—Peter and I had one of those, too. I'm confused about your husband, I must say. There. Greta has settled. Sometimes they're just looking for a warm sweater-vest to snuggle in. There is truly nothing like a small dog in one's lap.

—My husband, like you, wrote of Paul Bunyan. I wonder if you were taken, as he was, by a mythology so masculine and destructive. A man as big as a machine who plucks trees in the name of progress, who hangs out in a logging camp with a homosocial band of shirtless Swedes and whose best friend is an enormous blue ox. In your operetta, Paul gets married, okay, but he's lousy at it and his wife leaves camp with their daughter. The whole thing is a little too Gilbert and Sullivan for me, but there are gorgeous moments. I'm thinking of "Bunyan's Goodnight":

—Please. You won't sing it. Greta sleeps.

—No, okay, but Auden's libretto: "Now let the complex spirit dissolve in the darkness where the actual and the possible are mysteriously exchanged. Dear children, trust the night and have faith in tomorrow that these hours of ambiguity and indecision may be also the hours of healing." Those words set against your birdsong, the night birds, their minor and melancholic fade. I'm helped by that idea of night, the sound of that night.

—Wystan is a most consoling poet. Speaking of birds, what is that delightful sound I keep hearing.

—What sound?

—That one, the birds, I think, chortling and muttering. It's lovely, really, and I'd like to know what sort of bird makes that lovely sound. Over there, behind the hawthorn hedge. Hear it? Lovely, really.

—Chickens.

—No.

—Yes, they're very happy hens. They make that sound when they're happy and when no hawks circle.

—Really. How awfully fantastic. I envy chickens, you know.

—Why is that?

—Well, it's quite a naughty reason, really.

—Go ahead. I'm Canadian.

—Because if they feel like doing it, they do it.

—Those are hens, Benjamin, and they have no rooster. I believe only the rooster feels like doing it and will often not ask a hen's permission, and he'll do it so often and forcefully to whichever hen is proximate that the feathers are worn from her back and next morning she's last one out of the coop hoping he'll be too tired by the time she arrives. Lay an egg, beak a grub, flutter in dust: these are a hen's pleasures.

—I wonder: which instrument will I use to mimic that sound? Flutes would be too obvious. Something expressive of what you've just explained: the innocence and vulnerability . . .

—Aren't those the twin themes of all your work? Even the *War Requiem*?

—Clarinets may be too goose-like. I've solved these problems before, you know, many times. It once took me several days walking in the chapel to find a way to make a noise like bath water running out. I once used china mugs hung on a length of string hit with a wooden spoon to suggest first raindrops falling on the ark. It's almost like mathematics, is it not? Aeolian harp, perhaps, to express the way a hen's feathers are layered and firm, yet delicate and soft. A nice C major for purity and simplicity.

—One critic said that "Mr. Britten will have proved his worth as a composer when he succeeds in writing music that relies less on superficial effect."

—No friendliness – no encouragement – no perception. I was discouraged by such critics. Later, I was appreciated but not understood.

—What about the superficial effect?

—You know yourself that writing isn't that way, it doesn't happen that way. You get a sense of the whole work, and then you plan it, and you sit down and write it, and it takes charge, and it all goes to pieces, in my experience! You try and control it, and sometimes you succeed, but not always. As E.M. Forster writes, very wisely, in *Aspects of the Novel*, the work has to take over. One doesn't like it taking over, because it does things quite often that you don't like. But there is ... an inner compulsion that one does one's best to control.

—So superficial effects are the will of the material, rather than the ego of the artist?

—Artists are artists because they have an extra sensitivity – a skin less, perhaps, than other people; and the great ones have an uncomfortable habit of being right about many things, long before their time. So. When you hear of an artist saying or doing something strange and unpopular, think of that extra sensitivity – that skin less – before you condemn him. Ah, the self-doubting artist. What is the cure? It is not public acceptance, no. That is just another harness for the artist. What, oh dear god, what is that?

—Where are you looking?

—Your neighbour's field, riding on the mowing machine. Oh dear lord. Turn my chair, would you. Greta: Off! Off! Off! Oh dear, dear lord. There is something so compelling in the amoral landscape, don't you agree?

—He's twelve years old, Benjamin. His parents are accountants.

—Indeed, and look at the delicacy of the shoulders, or more precisely, where shoulder meets bicep. Were he to wear a shirt, those bones would not be so lovely, so profound in the lowering sun of early evening. A boy should always be just that way: his long torso made golden in late sun, his legs long in blue jeans astride an animal of growling power. Oh dear heaven. Total acceptance of the sensual, my dear, that is the goal of the artist. It's all spoiled somewhat by the ridiculous wires dangling from his ears, but nevertheless.

—He's twelve. He's listening to music. They all do that now. Music is constant companion and portable consolation. My daughter, in the months since her father betrayed her and moved to another family, to another daughter not his, to another farm nearby and its cliffs and wealth, my daughter healed her heart with Van Morrison's cheering early stuff, with

Queens of the Stone Age, with German death metal, with Frank Sinatra and Annie Lennox and "Do Ya Think I'm Sexy." I praise a culture that makes music so available, so portable, so private. My daughter has been saved, as I was, by the world's notes.

—Eclectic, indeed. It causes me great pain in my old murmering heart to think of your daughter's innocence before her father diminished it, and what must be her daily – no, hourly – struggle to both maintain what remains of it and to also reject the inadequacies of innocence. Innocence outraged. Will music be enough? I think not. I wish to write a ballet set in Australia – or maybe right here on southern Vancouver Island – I want to work out something to do with the Aboriginals. Western civilization is not bringing up its children properly, but the Aboriginals did. They reared their children to deal with life and be at one with it, and we haven't done that. We've got more kind of complicated and more difficult. I want to show two things simultaneously: the life of a boy growing up in an Australian Aboriginal tribe and the life of a boy growing up English. The English boy gets the tragic ending, of course. But with your daughter's suffering, perhaps, will come the capacity for art and therefore the promise of healing, if not peace.

—I find that comforting.

—Give me your hand to hold. Both hands. Rest your head against my knee. They replaced a valve in my heart, you know. An aortic homograft: human tissue grafted rather than a mechanical valve inserted. I was told that despite the best care in the world, some valves taken from humans let you down when transplanted into others. I was never the same. Bits of debris from the valve entered the circulation and one lodged in my brain. This caused a weakness in my right hand that prevented speed on the piano. I missed my walks, I missed swimming in the cold sea at night, badminton, skiing. I missed my body and its acts. I lost heart, I suppose. It isn't fun to feel like the wrong end of a broken down bus for most of the time. But people die at the right moment, and I believe I did. The greatness of a person includes the time when he was born and the time endured, but this is difficult to understand. Mmmmmmmm. I so like to feel your lovely hand through my hair like that. I believe I was a horse in a past incarnation.

91

And you kiss well for a woman. For a woman of your age. Total acceptance of the sensual, my dear, there along my neck. Yes. Thank-you. We are all so fragile, you see.

—I like what Leonard Bernstein said after your death: "Benjamin Britten was a man at odds with the world," he said. "It's strange, because on the surface Britten's music would seem to be decorative, positive, charming, but it's so much more than that. When you hear Britten's music, if you really hear it, not just listen to it superficially, you become aware of something very dark. There are gears that are grinding and not quite meshing, and they make a great pain." I think a singer knows this, and also that pain is made and pain is unmade in the singing.

—Night has fallen on us gently and it's time I left.

—Not yet.

—Yes, I'm afraid.

—Will I see you again?

—Oh dear. Please. Look at this garden of yours when those tears come. Think of your daughter and her music, your dog and her delight to have a woman like you at her side. Think of your work and, above all, continue. In "Curlew River," as the Traveller climbs into the boat, the cry of the Madwoman is heard as she approaches on the western side, accompanied by a bird-like flutter-tongued flute. Yes, she is tortured by sorrow, and still the leaping chromatic motif suggests not bereavement but excitement, and her words indicate she is trying to find the answer to a riddle:

Where the nest of the curlew
Is not filled with snow,
Where the eyes of the lamb
Are untorn by the crow,
There let me, there let me, there let me go!

—She doesn't sound like a Madwoman to me. She just needs a break from the landscape, a few days in the city, maybe see a hockey game or get a fancy haircut, new shoes.

—Indeed. She is not mad, but visionary. She will carry on and she will come back.

—This garden without you now? It matters to me that *you* come back, Benjamin.

—No, my dear girl, you must understand this, and so must your daughter and the boy next door, too, and your husband who should have known but chose to forget: sounding right, sounding right is all that matters.

Acknowledgments

These pieces are fictional in intent and execution, but I have made frequent use of secondary sources in order to convey with respect and authenticity the spirit – and sometimes the real-world words – of those "interviewed." Biographies, magazine articles, bits from newspapers, television interviews, online interviews in odd places like harryrosen.com, liner notes: these are only some of what I consulted for each interview before imagining it. A few call for special mention: when Alice Munro speaks of writing as "a fight against death," she is quoting herself in an interview conducted by Graeme Gibson, and the interviewer is quoting John Gould; Humphrey Carpenter's biography of Benjamin Britten was essential, as was Jim Hughson's interview with Markus Näslund on *Snapshots*; the work of Brian Pronger is alluded to in the Bobby Orr interview. Richard Ford's responses are taken verbatim from an interview I conducted with him by phone for *The Georgia Straight*, except his ideas about suicide, which are imagined; the questions he's asked in the story were not the same as those I asked. I borrow, too, from my own book, *Cold-cocked: On Hockey*.

Kind and helpful editors have published some of these stories in *Brick*, *The New Quarterly*, *Short Story*, *CNQ: Canadian Notes & Queries*. Ally Hack was a most meticulous researcher who now has a special place in her heart for Janet Jones-Gretzky. Thanks to John Metcalf and John Burns.

The British Columbia Arts Council provided funding at just the right time. Their support – and that of friends, colleagues and students – matters.

As always, Max Jackson.

PHOTO: www.diananethercott.com

Vancouver-raised **Lorna Jackson** began her working life as a musician and travelled throughout British Columbia for nine years as a bass player and singer. She has published a collection of short stories, *Dressing for Hope*, and a novel, *A Game To Play on the Tracks*. *Cold-cocked: On Hockey*, the first book to explore a woman's way of watching the game poet Al Purdy called a "combination of ballet and murder," was published by Biblioasis in 2007. As well, her non-fiction and literary journalism have appeared in *Brick*, *Quill & Quire*, *The Georgia Straight*, and *Malahat Review*. She teaches Writing at the University of Victoria.